LESSONS OF THE GAME

LESSONS OF THE GAME

Diane Gonzales Bertrand

PIÑATA BOOKS
ARTE PÚBLICO PRESS
HOUSTON, TEXAS
1998

This volume is made possible through grants from the National Endowment for the Arts (a federal agency), Andrew W. Mellon Foundation, and the City of Houston through The Cultural Arts Council of Houston, Harris County.

Piñata Books are full of surprises!

Piñata Books
An Imprint of Arte Público Press
University of Houston
Houston, Texas 77204-2174

Cover illustration and design by Giovanni Mora

Bertrand, Diane Gonzales.
    Lessons of the game / by Diane Gonzales Bertrand.
    p.   cm.
    Summary: Romance blossoms when student teacher Kaylene finds that the handsome Alex, a friend from her past, is a football coach at her new school, but she fears that his busy schedule will not let him spend any time with her.
    ISBN 1-55885-245-X (alk. paper)
    [1. Teachers—Fiction. 2. High schools—Fiction. 3. Schools—Fiction. 4. Football—Fiction.] I. Title.
PZ7.B46357Le   1998
[Fic]—dc21
                                         98-28340
                                               CIP
                                             AC

8 9 0 1 2 3 4 5 6 7   10 9 8 7 6 5 4 3 2 1

To
Mary Alice Bertrand
who loves me like a daughter
and to her son
Nick
who fills my life with love and laughter.

Chapter One

"Keep away from Ralph, or I'll rip your ugly face off!"

"Try it, you witch!"

A jaw-cracking slap whipped the air.

As Kaylene Morales reached the top step, she saw a black haired girl in a yellow dress slam a redhead with spiked hair into the lockers. The savage behavior astounded her. She had come to the second floor of Leon Creek High School to meet her supervising teacher. An after-school fight between two wildcats wasn't the ideal introduction to student teaching.

Looking up and down the hallway, Kaylene searched for someone to stop the girls. They spat fiery words and insults as they grappled together, their two bodies becoming a tornado of color. Purple nails twisted into frizzy black hair. White heels kicked into blue denim legs. Ripped yellow fabric whipped the crimson face with lightning green eyes.

Kaylene's hand raked her brunette hair as the female storm intensified. Sensing the danger if this hurricane continued, her dark brown eyes darted over the area for something to distract the girls. Then she saw the janitor's bucket and big gray mop outside a classroom.

Her legs wobbled after she grabbed the tin bucket and turned towards the girls. As Kaylene swung the bucket back, and threw its contents on the fighters, the water ricocheted off the lockers—dousing a man who had just run around the corner.

The unexpected shower stunned everyone. The redhead slipped down on one knee; the dressy one slid across the wet lockers. Wet stains splattered across the man's white shirt as foam dotted his green shorts and water dripped down his legs.

Kaylene dropped the bucket with a loud clang as she recognized the man in the soggy clothes. He choked back expletives as he wiped his face, then stiffly flicked the moisture away.

Kaylene couldn't believe it. She hadn't seen Alex Garrison in ten years, and their reunion was toasted with mop water.

"Alex!"

His glaring anger fizzled into disbelief as he recognized her. "Kaylene?"

"Coach, she threw the janitor's water on us!" The dark haired girl screeched. "She can't do that, can she?"

"Coach?" Kaylene's surprise increased. She quickly studied Alex. What had once been a short, average build now looked brawny and powerful. The white knit shirt stretching over his broad shoulders tapered down to his narrow waist. The green shorts permitted a liberal view of two tanned muscular legs. His physical training as an athletic coach gave him a far different image than the Alex she remembered.

"I smell like the toilet," the red-headed student growled, her spikes flushed away by the water.

"I bet we all smell that way," Alex replied, sending an unhappy scowl in Kaylene's direction.

Embarrassment burned through her. "I'm sorry," she said. "I just wanted to stop the fighting before someone got hurt."

His grayish green eyes widened as he said, "Sloshing soap water in the halls can be even more dangerous than two freshmen girls fighting. Next time, get some help, okay?"

The edge to his voice annoyed Kaylene. Her solution was messy, but it was effective. If she had let the girls continue fighting, things might be worse. How would Alex have stopped the cat fight?

"Let's go, ladies! I'll walk you to Mr. Zachary's office."

Alex's voice thundered into her thoughts. He sounded as if he was going to take her to see the vice-principal too.

"Coach, you can't turn us in now. School's over!" The girl who spoke pieced together remnants of her torn yellow sleeve.

"This is school property no matter what time it is. Next time you want to fight, pick another place. Let's go!" Alex paused, and looked back at Kaylene. "Find someone to clean up this mess."

Kaylene was ready to start a storm of her own. He couldn't order her around like a student. "I have an appointment right now!" As she caught the grin on the redhead, she realized her resistance set a poor example. She changed her tone immediately. "Once I take care of my business, I'll make sure this area gets cleaned up, even if I have to do it myself."

With a sarcastic curve to his lips, Alex's eyes swept over her. "In that outfit? I don't think so."

Kaylene glanced down. She was dressed in a blue linen suit with a white silk blouse. She knew it was too formal for the classroom, but she had wanted to make a good first impression with her supervising teacher.

"There's the janitor. I'll talk to him." Alex gave an angry sigh. "Come on, ladies. I'm late already!" His arm jutted out, pointing out the direction to the vice-principal's office.

With a tight grip on the shoulder strap of her black purse, Kaylene walked the other way, still fuming over Alex's tone of voice. If Alex weren't so concerned about himself, he might have noticed she wasn't the scrawny teenager he had known a long time ago.

3

By the time Kaylene walked the long hallway and found Room 209, she had suppressed her feelings behind a more professional demeanor. She paused outside the door, carefully smoothing her layered brown hair, which hung two inches past her shoulders. She took a deep breath, then rapped once on the door before entering.

An imposing woman with blonde hair twisted up in a top-knot stood at the desk arranging papers.

Kaylene guessed her new supervising teacher was in her forties and probably represented a strong mother-figure to her students. Maybe the students would see Kaylene as the smarter, older sister.

"Mrs. Dunn? I'm Kaylene Morales, your student teacher." She walked to the teacher's desk, quickly surveying the classroom with its colorful posters and student work displayed on a large bulletin board. Tall open windows allowed a steady breeze to cool the room. Ash trees dotted with autumn colors waved outside.

"Hello, Kaylene, I'm Frances Dunn." Her blue eyes never left Kaylene's face as they shook hands. "I understand you're a graduate student at St. Mary's. Are you prepared to face the teenagers in my class?"

"Yes, Mrs. Dunn." Kaylene's stomach churned. She hadn't been prepared for the two girls' fighting in the hall. What else would surprise her? "Leon Creek was my first choice for student teaching, Mrs. Dunn."

"Even though Leon Creek is small compared to other San Antonio schools, we have our own challenges. I hope you know how to handle teenagers. I'll expect you to maintain control in my classroom."

Kaylene's confidence wavered as she looked up to the tall, older woman. Discipline was a serious part of teaching. She saw Alex's authority go unchallenged by the two girls only a few moments ago, and she assumed Mrs. Dunn had little trouble keeping her students under control. Kaylene needed to discover her own way of handling teenagers. She had already learned a janitor's bucket wasn't a practical way to solve problems.

Mrs. Dunn moved back to the desk, and reached for a teacher's plan book. "Now, I insist my student teachers follow the units I've mapped out for each semester. We can discuss specific methods and activities later. Let's see, if you start next week—" She paused to turn a few pages. "That'll put you teaching the last unit on connectives, six-weeks exams, and doing the Shakespeare unit. We're teaching *Romeo and Juliet*. Typical freshmen studies." She looked at Kaylene. "You'll observe tomorrow and begin teaching Monday."

Kaylene blinked in surprise. Her graduate classes moved so informally, she had been spoiled by the pace. She wanted answers to a hundred questions first. Instead, Mrs. Dunn handed her the keys and wanted her to jump behind the steering wheel.

Kaylene forced her fears into the back seat. She'd deal with each bump in the road as it appeared. "I'll be here tomorrow, Mrs. Dunn."

"Good, I—" Mrs. Dunn stopped at the loud knock on her door.

Kaylene turned around to see Alex step into the classroom. She couldn't believe they were reunited again, although the circumstances weren't much better than before.

"You're late, Coach," Mrs. Dunn commented in a dry voice. "I expected you ten minutes ago."

"Two girls were fighting in the halls." Alex halted when he saw Kaylene, but turned his face towards Mrs. Dunn. "I had to take them to Mr. Zachary."

Mrs. Dunn frowned. "Is it raining outside, Coach?"

Kaylene saw the embarrassed blush tint Alex's face as he glanced down at his water-stained shirt and shorts. Although he stood about six feet from them, she could smell the pine cleaner still fresh on his clothes. She looked at the tiled floor, waiting for Alex to implicate her in the commotion which had made him late.

"The janitor's bucket toppled over during the fight," he said, his voice sounding as if the incident wasn't even worth mentioning.

Kaylene was grateful for his chivalry. A touch of the old Alex had surfaced at last, and she looked up to smile at him.

"May we talk now?" Alex asked Mrs. Dunn.

She was hurt that he ignored her to get his job done.

"Coach, I know you want to talk to me, but my student teacher was here first."

Mrs. Dunn gestured towards Kaylene.

"I should have been on the field twenty minutes ago. I can't afford to delay practice any longer," Alex told her. "If your student teacher won't mind—"

"Really, Mrs. Dunn," Kaylene interjected. "I don't mind if you talk to Alex."

"Do you know Coach Garrison?"

Mrs. Dunn's direct look made Kaylene's face warm.

"He went to school with my brother." She didn't want to admit the topic of Alex Garrison had filled a diary when she was twelve. But she didn't really know this Alex, not this man others called Coach.

"Mrs. Dunn, you need to change the day your book report is due," Alex blurted out.

Kaylene's eyes widened. Did he *always* roll right over people to get his point across?

Crossing his arms across his chest, Alex continued. "My freshmen boys have worked hard all week preparing for their first game. They're worried about the book report due Friday. Can you let them turn it in on Monday?"

"Why should I give a handful of athletes special treatment?"

"I"d like you to change your deadline for your whole class, not just my athletes."

Kaylene admired Alex's cool determination. He never broke eye contact with Mrs. Dunn.

"You know, it bothers me when coaches expect teachers to change deadlines because of a football game. My late husband was a coach, so I know it's tough on the athletes to get everything done. But my book report is just as important as your football game."

Kaylene studied Alex, wondering what kind of coach he'd become. Was he more concerned about winning his first game, or the needs of his players?

"I can't argue with your logic," he said. "But these boys are just freshmen. Can't we work together so they can do their best at football and give you a decent book report too?"

"Why must teachers in the classroom compromise so coaches can have their way?" She shook her head slowly. "My book report deadline stands. If I were you, I'd let the athletes leave practice early so they can do their book report."

Fire blazed in Alex's eyes, but he straightened his shoulders, uncrossed his arms, and nodded with complete control. His voice was clear and cold. "Thank you for your time, Mrs. Dunn. I'll get back to my boys now."

"Wait, Coach." Mrs. Dunn's order stopped Alex's departure. She stepped aside, motioning to Kaylene. "Tell me, Ms. Morales. Would you change the deadline to Monday?"

As Alex gave Kaylene his full attention for the first time, blood rushed to her head, heating up her face.

"It depends," Kaylene croaked, then cleared her throat. She mustered her confidence just as she had when she confronted the wildcats fighting in the hall. "When did you make the assignment?"

"Two weeks ago, Thursday." Mrs. Dunn's voice rang with the confidence of someone who believed she was right.

Kaylene looked at Alex, whose watchful stare sparkled with emotions she couldn't comprehend. Did he resent her involvement in this discussion? Did he expect her to side with him because she knew him years ago? She knew the assignment and deadline were not unfair.

She looked back at Mrs. Dunn. She didn't want to hurt Alex, but her supervising teacher's respect would be influenced by this decision. "Two weeks is more than enough time to complete an assignment, Mrs. Dunn. The students knew about your deadline long before Alex—I mean, Coach Garrison—began practice for his first game."

Mrs. Dunn raised one blonde eyebrow as she looked back at Alex. "Ms. Morales seems to agree with me, Coach."

Lips pressed together, he nodded. A shadow of disappointment in his eyes made Kaylene soften with guilt. And even though she knew three extra days would be welcome by all the students who procrastinated, she couldn't show favoritism towards Alex and the athletes so early in her teaching career.

"Then the matter's settled. Good afternoon!" Alex quietly spun on the heels of his white leather shoes. Pride and anger seemed to stiffen his walk as he left the two women alone in the classroom.

"Yes, that matter's settled," Mrs. Dunn murmured, then looked at Kaylene. "It doesn't matter when you set the deadline, Kaylene, just that you stick to it. The students need to realize the importance of deadlines, something we all have to learn to live with."

Kaylene shrugged, voicing her thoughts. "Sometimes, though, a little extra time adds quality to a project."

"Is that what you really think? That the book reports will be better if I read them Monday night?"

"Maybe—" Kaylene turned to face Mrs. Dunn, raising her eyes in a steady look. "Really, it's a gamble. Right now I bet all the athletes can think about is football. After the game, they can concentrate on something else. A book report, I hope."

"But there are other games. Do I change deadlines the rest of the season?"

8

"No, Mrs. Dunn. Just keep the schedule in mind while you're planning."

Kaylene chewed on her lip wishing she could call back her words. The last thing she wanted was to sound like she had all the answers.

Mrs. Dunn walked back to the desk with heavy steps. "Considering you'll be teaching the rest of the football season, I suggest you follow your own advice. I'll see you tomorrow, Ms. Morales. I teach all periods except third." She didn't look up, as she said, "Good-bye."

"Good-bye, Mrs. Dunn. I'll be here for first period."

Kaylene left the room quietly, but her thoughts boomed inside her head. Nothing she had faced today was in any education textbook. After the six-week program was complete, maybe she'd write her own book on teaching, with a special chapter on diplomatic relations with coaches. A little voice was warning Kaylene that she hadn't seen the last of Alex Garrison.

——∽∾——

Alex slammed down the release bar of the glass door as he stalked out the side door of the main building. He stomped down the sidewalk, heading for the Leon Creek gymnasium, the red brick building in the rear of the school property.

Kaylene Morales! Where had she come from? He hadn't seen the girl in years, and suddenly, she had unknowingly sabotaged his carefully planned meeting with Mrs. Dunn.

He wanted to be prompt, professional, and persuasive. Thanks to Kaylene, he smelled like the men's room, sounded like just another coach begging for favors, and stuck around long enough to look like a fool twice. He couldn't believe Kaylene sided with the old bat, especially after he didn't mention she was to blame for his wet clothes.

9

As he reached the rear of the gymnasium, Alex knew he'd have to do some real motivation work if he wanted his boys to pass Mrs. Dunn's English class.

"Hey, Coach! Watch out!"

Alex grunted as helmets grazed his shoulders and padded bodies roughly shoved him aside. Loud curses rippled over the endless tide of athletes tumbling out of the gym door. As the boys crunched over his feet, Alex tried to sidestep them, but instead fell backwards. Luckily, three pairs of hands latched onto him. He gripped onto the nearest football player to get his balance, then pushed himself away, avoiding any further contact. He stood by the door, trying to steady his breathing.

Domingo Reyes, the other freshman coach, was the last one out. Grinning, he tossed Alex his baseball cap. "Have a death wish? Once I blow that whistle, nothing but a brick wall will stop our freshmen!"

Alex shoved the green cap over his short, curly brown hair. "You should have been on the field thirty minutes ago."

"You said you'd be back in fifteen minutes. I went over the new offensive plays. The time wasn't wasted," Domingo replied with a shrug. He didn't seem fazed by Alex's mood.

"I wasted *my* time. That's for sure." Alex took his clipboard from Domingo and glanced over today's practice schedule.

Domingo fell into step beside Alex as they walked towards the football field. "Dunn wouldn't budge, huh?"

"No way! Then, her student teacher put her two cents in, and the idea got shot down again!"

"Student teacher? Does she have great legs?"

Alex's head shot up to discover the wide grin on his assistant's tanned face.

"Sorry, I didn't notice her legs." The silly question helped relax him. "Actually, I knew the woman. Well, I knew her when she was a little girl." He cleared his throat, not wanting to admit Kaylene had caught his attention at all. He didn't have time to think about anything but football right now.

Domingo slapped him on the shoulder. "Well, I'm glad you noticed that much. Usually, you don't talk much about women."

"Right now, the game is football, not love." Alex glanced at the players falling into line for warm-up exercises. He enjoyed his career, and knew it would take a special woman to understand his commitment to Texas's number one sport. After the last woman deserted him mid-season, he wasn't going to pay attention to another until well after the team hung up its helmets. Especially a little girl who had blossomed into an attractive student teacher.

When Domingo blew his whistle, Alex brought his thoughts back to the job at hand. Domingo was head track coach, but he preferred the role of freshman assistant coach in football. Pressure always fell upon Alex from the head coach, David Maldonado, to instill a winning attitude in the boys who would be his future varsity.

As Alex surveyed the rows of athletes going through the warm-up drills, he realized everyone had come a long way since that first morning of Two-A-Days, practice at 7 a.m. and again at 4 p.m. every day for the last two weeks in August. A group of misfits with leftover cocky eighth grade superiority, Alex retrained them in the Maldonado style of football, and now they worked as a team, aiming for the same goal post.

Alex knew from experience that the most important touchdowns in life required dedication, commitment, and sacrifice. If he could impart his philosophy to his athletes, they'd always come out winners.

—∿∿—

As Kaylene sat at the rear of Mrs. Dunn's classroom, she was very curious about the boy reading. His larger than typical fifteen-year-old size, mature good looks, and gleaming white football jersey caught her attention almost immediately when he entered fourth period. When Mrs. Dunn called him Ralph, Kaylene couldn't help but wonder if he was the boy who caused yesterday's hallway hurricane.

Now Kaylene admired Mrs. Dunn's patient look while others shifted in desks uncomfortably or sighed. Her blue eyes attended to Ralph as if he read Poe like a polished actor. When he painstakingly reached the end of the paragraph, she told him, "Thank you, Ralph. You read well."

Four jersey-clad boys near the center of the room snickered loudly. Mrs. Dunn silenced them with a stare.

"Even though you aren't on the football field, I'd expect you boys to always support your teammates, not ridicule them."

Someone coughed, another shrugged his shoulders, and the others didn't budge. Kaylene promised herself to practice such a look in the mirror before she began teaching on Monday.

"Edgar Allan Poe is difficult even for experienced readers," Mrs. Dunn told the class. "Ralph did a fair job considering the language. Tell me, Ralph, what do you think of the narrator?"

The boy who sat by the windows smoothed his black hair. "I think he's a psycho! He killed his boss, the guy with one eye. Now he hears things because he feels guilty." One long, brown finger tapped his temple. "But it's all in here."

Mrs. Dunn tilted her head, a slight smile on her lips. "You've got the main idea, Ralph. Good job."

Ralph grunted triumphantly at his fellow players, then quickly snapped his middle finger alongside his dark hair as a nonverbal reply to their laughter.

Although the vulgar gesture shocked Kaylene, Mrs. Dunn's large face remained professionally cold.

"Ralph, keep your opinions to yourself. Keisha, continue to read."

As the young black girl continued Poe's story in a clear, expressive voice, Kaylene returned her attention to the notes she made during the morning classes. She noted Ralph and his athlete friends' behavior for future reference.

Fourth period ended as Keisha finished reading the story. Kaylene watched the students noisily bound from the room before she moved to the front of the classroom.

Mrs. Dunn glanced up from her position behind the desk. "Lunch continues until 11:55. I usually eat a sandwich in the lounge. Do you know where the cafeteria is, Ms. Morales?"

"I'll be back in time for fifth period, Mrs. Dunn." Kaylene slipped her purse under her arms. As she left the classroom, she tried not to let Mrs. Dunn's attitude depress her. After spending the conference period together, she accepted that Mrs. Dunn wasn't a friendly person. She did her job well and expected the same from others. She pointed out requirements, explained rules, and answered Kaylene's questions, but never moved outside professional bounds, even to ask Kaylene why she wanted to be a teacher.

Students grabbing their belongings from their lockers dotted the hall. Doors slammed, girls squealed over a list on a bulletin board, and boys chuckled suggestively nearby. Kaylene followed a group of students downstairs to the cafeteria.

The food smells seeped through the large aluminum windows dividing the cafeteria from the hall. She pulled open the door, and looked around in puzzled amazement.

The cafeteria was as big as a gymnasium. Long formica-topped tables with aluminum legs and attached benches covered tiled floors. Soft drink and snack machines lined one wall, and the L-shaped counter serving hot food absorbed the other walls.

She tried to decide between smells of tacos, pizza, and hamburgers and the mystery meat smothered in gravy she saw students carrying on their trays. The noisy confusion of the place and clanging of pans distracted her. She looked around, and saw several men patrolling the cafeteria. She smiled as she spied one familiar face in the sea of strangers.

Alex stood near the soda machines, his arms crossed across his broad chest as he watched the students. He was professionally attired in a green shirt and black slacks. Her heart pounded as she moved towards him, hoping he wouldn't run in the other direction when he saw her.

His gaze softened when their eyes met and Kaylene hoped for a smile to welcome her.

"Teachers usually use the other entrance. They have a separate dining room." Alex said, in a voice easily carrying over the din.

She wondered why Alex always managed to shake up her confidence. Kaylene shrugged. "Sorry, I didn't know."

His light brown eyebrows raised. "Actually, no teacher comes in here unless its a matter of life or death."

She smiled, but Alex's professional mask was still in place. She guessed he was still angry about yesterday's unfortunate circumstances. "I'd like to apologize, Alex."

"For throwing mop water at me, or siding with Mrs. Dunn?"

Kaylene sighed. "The water thing was an accident. And as for Mrs. Dunn, I couldn't go against her. She's my supervising teacher." She wished he'd stop just once, and think about things from her point of view.

"I'm really looking forward to dealing with a younger version of Mrs. Dunn the rest of the semester."

"I'm nothing like Mrs. Dunn." Kaylene said, trying to match the look Mrs. Dunn gave her students in class today.

Alex took a step back, his hand rubbing his chin. "I'm sure you're not, Kaylene."

Kaylene shoved her hands into the side pockets of her red skirt. "And if we're going to work with the same students, I hope you'll remember I'm a teacher, not one of the kids."

"What does that mean?"

"I mean the way you talk to me. In case you haven't noticed, I'm not fourteen years old anymore."

"I noticed, Kaylene." His eyes looked darker because of the moss-colored shirt he wore. "Actually, if we had met under any other circumstances, I would have enjoyed catching up on the last ten years."

Kaylene wondered if she'd have a friend on the faculty after all. "I'll be here for the next six weeks. Maybe we can talk again."

Alex shook his head. "Don't count on it. I don't have much free time during football season."

The one person at Leon Creek who might have been a friend had brushed her aside. Again. "Sure, Alex. I understand. Bye."

Distance seemed to be the name of the game at this school, and she could be just as cool and professional as everyone else. She turned around and decided to just skip lunch.

"Kaylene?"

She turned at his call, steadying herself for more bad news. "Yes?"

"If any of my athletes give you any trouble, let me know, okay?" His mouth curved into an unconscious smile. "I bet they'll enjoy watching you instead of Mrs. Dunn for the next six weeks."

Kaylene's dark eyes blinked in amazement. Was there actually a charming man underneath the gruff coach? She wasn't prepared for the sudden change in his voice, the warm caress of his eyes. She calmly nodded, and left him to his job.

As she walked through the noisy cafeteria, Kaylene decided Leon Creek High School would have more challenges than she had anticipated, and each one deserved her careful attention.

Chapter Two

Navy blue skies streaked by purple clouds had set the backdrop for the Friday night football drama. Enthusiastic football fans electrified Edgewood Stadium with a power stronger than the lights beaming down on the field. Band instruments played warm-up notes, and pep squad girls dressed in identical uniforms rocked side to side as they chanted a rhyming cheer about victory for the Raiders.

Clutching the front guardrail of the stadium, Kaylene pressed herself against it to let three teenage girls pass her in the narrow row. She walked along, glancing towards the rectangular wooden house at the top of the stadium. Her university friends said they'd be sitting near the press box. She paused to let a little boy scamper by, his hand squeezed tight around a dill pickle. She started up the cement steps but hesitated so that a fat man could come down first. Finally, she began the climb up, skimming over faces in search of her friends.

Nothing familiar caught her attention as she stopped a few steps below the press box. Pausing to catch her breath, she noticed the row of men adjusting binoculars, straightening papers within clipboards, or testing pens on the back of yellow legal pads. Why would anyone need a pen and paper at a football game?

Kaylene's eyebrows raised as she spotted Alex Garrison sitting close by. Talking to a heavy-set, bearded man, Alex pointed to something on a clipboard. As she noticed Alex's green cap with LC embroidered on it, she saw others wore shirts or caps branded with school insignia. They were all coaches from other teams watching their competition.

After Alex's semi-friendly parting message in the cafeteria today, Kaylene decided to risk a hello, then find her friends. As she made her way down the empty row directly in front, she heard one coach wolf-whistle under his breath. She grinned before she called out, "Alex! Hello!"

Alex looked up. "Kaylene? What are you doing here?" His eyebrows tilted in a frown.

Kaylene heard the impatience in his voice. "I'm here with friends. Linda is student teaching at Edgewood." She hoped he'd realize she didn't want to bother him. She turned away and studied the crowd hoping to spot Linda's red hair.

"If you're going to stay here, you'll have to sit down." Alex's commanding tone forced her attention back to him.

Suddenly, the crowd stood up, waving arms, shaking paper streamers and cheering loudly. Each team tore through its school spirit banner. An enthusiastic football team and pretty cheerleaders cheered and hollered as they took their places on the field.

Kaylene saw the coaches begin taking notes, study printed football programs, and use the binoculars for a closer look at the teams.

Rapidly, Alex explained something to the bearded man, ignoring Kaylene completely.

She sighed when she finally saw her friends sitting six rows down. She glanced back at Alex, who seemed to be completely focused on the football field.

"I see my *friends*," she said, emphasizing the last word. If she treated her friends the way he did, she wouldn't have any.

18

Alex handled his black binoculars, smoothing the strap around his neck. "That's good."

Kaylene watched the busy men who could think of nothing but football. She hated to think of Alex possessing such a one-track mind.

"Kaylene, you need to sit down," he repeated.

She glared back. "I'm joining the women I came with. Good-bye, Alex."

He nodded, then put the binoculars up to his eyes. "Okay, Eric. Pro-right, split backs."

She saw the man beside him diagram something on a white paper printed with circles.

Kaylene quickly weaved down the bleachers as a whistle sounded and the crowd cheered the kick-off. Irritated by Alex's rejection, she promised herself not to give him another thought, and smiled warmly at her friends.

"We thought you got lost," Linda said, brushing a strand of red hair back from her face.

"Actually, you were the lost ones." Kaylene sat beside Audrey, a dark-haired woman with glasses. "When I went off to the ladies room, I forgot I'd have to find you among all these people."

"So, Linda," Carla interrupted. "Which coach is the one you teach next-door to?" She sat on the other side of Audrey.

Planting her hands on her thighs, Linda leaned forward to study the coaches dressed in identical red shirts standing among the row of players on the sidelines. "It's hard to tell from up here. Too bad we don't have binoculars!"

Kaylene glanced back towards the press box. She searched for Alex behind his pair of field glasses. Her face warmed as she realized his binoculars pointed in her direction. Quickly she snapped her head towards the field, wondering why he would be watching her instead of the game. Could Alex Garrison actually be just a little curious about her?

19

At half-time, Kaylene purposely didn't go downstairs with her friends for a soda, just in case Alex might come by. So when he did appear, Kaylene decided to give him a dose of his own medicine.

"Don't coaches work at half-time too?" The chilly sound in her voiced pleased her.

Alex sat beside her, and Kaylene self-consciously scooted over. His clean-smelling aftershave tempted her to welcome his attention, but her brain reminded her of his unpredictable moods.

"Tonight I'm just scouting," Alex told her. "At half-time, scouts eat two bowls of nachos smothered in jalapeños. I'm holding out for something better." He slid closer to her.

The apparent game of pursuit made her heart race.

Alex leaned forward, one elbow resting on his thigh. "You know, Kaylene, we keep running into each other at the wrong times. I'd love to find some free time to talk to you."

"If I recall, you said you didn't have any free time during football season." She enjoyed using his own words against him.

"Yeah, I did say that, didn't I?" His deep chuckle softened her resolve. She finally looked at him.

She had always been attracted to his eyes. They blended the fresh green of springtime with a smoky warmth. The years had molded a strong, handsome face from his boyish teenage features.

"Let's catch up on the last ten years, Kaylene. You need to come with me for a pizza after the game."

"You have a bad habit of ordering people around. Do you know that?" she scolded him, concealing her excitement over the unexpected invitation.

With a lopsided grin, Alex shrugged. "It gets the job done."

"So does the word *please*."

In a smooth, quick movement Alex took her hand and squeezed it gently. "Please? Will you please go out with me after the game?"

Kaylene's resistance melted at the sight of her small hand nestled into his large one. She couldn't remember when such a simple gesture made her feel so desirable.

Before she could reply, a thought had reshaped his eyebrows.

"Kaylene, will your friends mind?"

"I'll explain it all. They'll understand." She realized she had agreed to go with him without even saying yes.

—◊◊◊—

As Alex started his navy blue Cutlass, he glanced over at Kaylene, who brushed her fingers over the leather seat cover.

"Nice car," she said. "Whatever happened to the white Ford?"

Alex laughed. "You remember that car?"

"Sure I do. Thanks to the noisy muffler, Daddy always knew when you brought Pat home."

"So how's Pat doing? He's still in El Paso?" Alex asked as he drove his car into the post-game traffic.

"Yes. He and Marissa have two daughters." Kaylene giggled. "I get my revenge through his girls for all the times Pat was mean to me. I gave them toy drums and squeaky horns last Christmas."

Spots of street lights decorated the car interior. Even in the darkness, Alex noticed her animated face as she spoke further about her nieces. His eyes drifted past layers of dark brown hair to the feminine curves under her white sweater. He marveled that a skinny, freckle-faced kid had developed such interesting attributes.

21

When she stopped talking, he realized he hadn't heard a word she said. He realized he didn't want to know more about Pat and his family, but about Kaylene and her life.

"Which university do you attend?" he asked, hoping she didn't know he changed the subject to conceal his inattentiveness.

"St. Mary's University. I should have worked on teacher certification sooner, but I got a chance to study in Mexico a year. I've got several ideas for a thesis, but right now, it's on the back burner until I finish student teaching. I need to get a full-time job." Kaylene met his glance. "And you, Alex? What have you been up to the past ten years?"

Alex shrugged. "School. Work. The usual. I started teaching and coaching five years ago. This is my first year at Leon Creek."

"Tell me what I can expect from the kids, Alex." Kaylene shifted so she looked directly at him. "You coach freshmen. Do you teach freshmen too?"

Alex noted the anxiety in her voice. He wished he had the answers she wanted, but each new teacher faced her own set of problems. "I teach P.E. at all levels, Kaylene. I get a different perspective on the kids than the classroom teachers. Overall, the kids are pretty friendly. I'm sure no one will do anything you can't handle." He gave her a wink. "You already know how to stop a fight between two girls."

"You didn't think I had such a great idea yesterday!"

Alex cleared his throat. "I was on my way to a meeting with Mrs. Dunn. I was angry at the inconvenience, not your methods. Actually, the way you stopped the fight wasn't *too* crazy. I never like to get between two screaming fighters, especially the girls."

"Do I detect a touch of chauvinism?"

"Maybe. Too many long fingernails and biting teeth for me!"

Kaylene's amused laughter filled the car. "Me too."

Alex relaxed into the seat as the genial conversation continued. A tiny voice warned him not to grow accustomed to the warm feelings Kaylene stirred within him. He had learned his bitter lesson last season, and knew these moments had to be only a short interlude, not a permanent fixture in his busy schedule.

—⁂—

The pizza restaurant's dim lighting added to the sense of privacy Kaylene enjoyed with Alex. Grateful for the quiet, half-empty room, she knew they'd have a better chance to re-acquaint themselves.

A gum-smacking teenager dressed in black pants and a checkered shirt that matched the tablecloth came up to the table. Leaning her weight into one hip, she took down their order on a little pad, before moving on, her gum snapping loudly.

"After a game, I usually eat alone. This is a nice change," Alex commented, leaning back in the wooden chair.

Kaylene nodded as she thought about her usual options for a Friday night: eating back at her apartment with her canary, or fast food with her friends. Sharing a pizza with a handsome man was the best alternative. Realizing she hadn't commented, but merely stared at him, she said the first thing that popped into her mind. "Do you like coaching?"

"I love coaching the athletes, and teaching them new ways to win, but the career has some drawbacks. When I'm not coaching the freshmen team, I'm working for the varsity coaches. It's a time-consuming job."

"Tonight, when I saw all those coaches from other schools watching, I was a little surprised. What's going on?"

"Well, each team sends out scouts who write down plays. We watch the better players who might cause problems for our defense. We study plays, how they're executed, and if one player dominates them. I watch a team three times before I write up my report for my head coach."

"I'm amazed at the amount of preparation done for a high school game, Alex."

"Coaches take their football very seriously in Texas, Kaylene. I work for a man who's trying to build up a weak program. Leon Creek hasn't had a winning season in five years. My head coach is dedicated seven days a week. He expects nothing less from his staff." His tired sigh reminded Kaylene of a steam whistle signaling the end of a work day. "I spend Thursday, Friday, and Saturday nights scouting. Then, I coach my own freshmen weekdays. I have seven scheduled games on Saturday mornings during the season. On Sunday, all the coaches go over the scouting reports and prepare for the next game."

Kaylene shook her head. His schedule made her feel tired just to think of all the responsibilities he carried on those ever-so-broad shoulders.

Alex moved his arm across the back of her chair. "I eat and sleep football during the season." Gently, his fingers walked up and down her arm.

His touch sent a spiral of heat to her toes. Her heartbeat quickened when his voice lowered.

"If you want a real test of faith, Kaylene, fall in love with a coach."

Kaylene turned to find his face only inches from hers. Was he making a joke? Teasing her with a dare, or issuing a warning? Who was this man sitting close enough to kiss her? She wanted to know everything about Alex. But when would Alex have time to be anything but a coach?

"One pepperoni pizza and two cokes," the waitress announced behind them.

Kaylene moved away as Alex dropped his arm. As the waitress set the steaming pizza between them, Kaylene decid-

24

ed she wouldn't think beyond the needs of her stomach. "This looks great! I'm starving!"

On the ride home, she talked about her parents' work in Laredo, the convenience of living within walking distance of St. Mary's University, and her canary. He talked about his parents, who traveled cross country in a motor home during the autumn months, and about his plans to attend his high school reunion next summer.

The pleasant evening finally ended outside the white duplex where Kaylene lived, a yellow light shining between the front doors.

"Thanks for the pizza, Alex," Kaylene said, leaning against the wooden porch railing.

Alex waited on the sidewalk, fingering his keys. "I'm glad we got a chance to talk."

Kaylene smiled at him. "Me too. Maybe we'll run into each other sometime at Leon Creek."

"Yeah, maybe so."

Kaylene's heart fluttered. "Maybe" was a step above "I'm too busy." She dropped her gaze, as she pulled her keys from her back pocket. "Good luck on your game tomorrow."

"Thanks." He cleared his throat. "Well, good night."

Kaylene spoke a soft "Good night," and turned to go up the steps. She heard the tapping of Alex's shoes on the sidewalk. She had just opened the screen door, when she heard Alex's clear call cutting through the late night stillness.

"Kaylene! Come to my game tomorrow morning!"

She turned to see him standing by his car. He was half-turned towards her, but she could see his smile.

Standing in the wedge of the open screen door, she merely laughed. "Say *please* and I'll be there for sure!"

He laughed too before he answered. "Please! Please? Why don't you come?"

Even though she didn't know much about football, seeing Alex work as coach piqued her curiosity. Besides, he did say "Please."

"Where and what time?" she called back.

"Leon Creek. Behind the gym. Ten o'clock."

"I'll be there. Maybe I can find a pom-pom!" She waved, then turned around to unlock her door. She greeted her canary, Tempest, who chirped and whistled at her appearance.

Kaylene didn't allow herself the pleasure of thinking about Alex and their evening together until she had turned out lights in the living room, changed into her favorite satin nightshirt, and settled herself upon the ivory-colored comforter of her bed.

She picked up the small tattered diary off the oak nightstand, which matched the old-fashioned headboard of the double bed. She smiled to herself, thinking it a funny coincidence that she found the diary this afternoon. She had rummaged through boxes in her closet, looking for a book on Shakespeare she wanted to use at Leon Creek.

> *I couldn't believe it. Alex noticed me.*
> *Alex gave me a button to wear to school.*
> *It says,* Braces are cool. *He touched my*
> *hand, and my heart jumped. He told me*
> *not to worry about the kids making fun*
> *of me. Someday, my smile would be*
> *perfect. He's so nice to me. I want to*
> *marry him.*

Kaylene put her fingers between the pages, and held the pink diary to her shoulder. In junior high, she had felt so ugly in braces, but for that one moment, Alex had made her feel pretty. He had a good way of finding positive aspects in not-so-pleasant things.

Yesterday, she had thought he had changed a lot, but now that she had spent time alone with him, she knew his friendliness and warmth were still a part of him. Now he concealed the personable qualities behind a serious professional mask. She had to respect Alex for taking his responsibilities so seriously, but she also knew there was a personal side to Alex she liked very much. It wasn't until she read through the diary that she remembered how strong her crush on Alex had been. Tonight, she felt a long-forgotten rush of excitement when they were together, especially when he asked her to come to his first game. She hoped there would be more opportunities to see Alex. She liked the way he made her feel. Then and now.

The next morning at the game, Kaylene's attention shifted from the football players to Alex pacing the sidelines of the grass field. His green coach's shirt was a beacon in the sea of white jerseys. She assumed he wore it so he could be seen easily among the bigger athletes. She wished she could see its effect on his eyes, which always changed shades whenever he wore green. From her position in the bleachers she couldn't see anything as intriguing as his eyes. All she saw or heard were hand gestures to a player to reposition himself or his loud, deep call. Frustration tensed his muscular frame when his players reached the ten-yard line several times, but they couldn't score.

Kaylene was impressed by Alex's style of coaching. He didn't scream at his players in anger, or call them names. He clapped his hands when his team did something right, and yelled out his approval. She could see he cared about his team as much as he did about winning.

—∽—

Alex looked at his team kneeling or sitting in a semi-circle around him and Domingo. "Guys, we need to work harder.

Concentrate. Remember what your job is and do it! The Central team isn't any better than you are. We still have the second half to go. We're going to have the ball first, so let's drive it down the field and score." He clapped his hands together three times. "Let's go, Wildcats! Let's go!"

His team responded with interjecting phrases and yells. They wiggled their sweaty heads back into their helmets. Then the freshmen jogged behind Alex and Domingo ready to begin the second half.

The game ended 3-0 when the Central field-goal kicker surprised everyone as his thirty-yard attempt sailed between the goalposts in the last seconds of the game.

Alex wasn't too hard on his boys in his post-game talk. He pointed out a defensive success since Central couldn't score a touchdown. He mentioned weak areas on the offense that needed to be corrected so the team could score next week. Then he sent the boys into the gym for their showers.

As he and Domingo followed the boys off the field, Alex glanced up the five row set of wooden bleachers. He saw Kaylene standing there. The breeze caught her brown hair and lifted it from her pensive face. Her presence there reminded him of the boost he had received as a boy whenever his parents came to watch him play ball. He always felt better knowing someone sat in the stands just for his sake, win or lose. Those warm feelings made him smile at Kaylene. She responded with a smile and a wave of her fingers.

Alex wished he had the time to speak to her, but he was needed elsewhere.

Domingo said something about Raymond, and Alex forced his attention back to his assistant. They entered the gym discussing the game, but soon went their separate ways. Domingo left to supervise the storing of the equipment and Alex headed for the coaches' office.

Alex wanted to turn around and leave when he spied his head coach, David Maldonado, leafing through a catalog. He leaned against the edge of Alex's desk. David's tall, dark looks always reminded Alex of a proud chief who led his fighting warriors towards victory.

Alex didn't feel too bad about today's loss since there was more luck than skill involved. He wasn't sure, though, how David would react.

"Good game, Coach," David told him, looking up. He closed the catalog, tossed it on the desk, and extended his hand.

Alex's eyebrow shot up. He wasn't expecting the praise. He accepted his boss' firm handshake. "Thanks, David. I appreciate you coming to the game."

"Your boys played well. First game jitters hurt you more than anything," he told Alex. "That three points was just a lucky break for Central." His voice lowered. "Would you mind a suggestion? I think it might help next week."

David's quiet manner shocked Alex. Usually a head coach offered his opinion whether you wanted to hear it or not.

"Sure, David. What's on your mind?"

"I think I would switch fourteen with sixteen. Sixteen moves quicker. I think he might give your quarterback more time to throw." As his gaze met Alex's glance, David shrugged. "It's just a suggestion, Alex. Talk it over with Domingo. Try it out at practice."

Alex rubbed his chin. He knew others often spot a weakness from a different vantage point. David had suggested his opinion from watching the game near the end zone. Actually, Alex had been thinking about rotating Cesar and Raymond himself.

"Your idea might work, David. Thanks."

David shoved his hands deep into his pockets of his coaching shorts. He rocked back on his heels. "I don't want you to scout Memorial after all. Kerrville's playing in Alamo Stadium and I'd like you there. I think they're going to be our biggest challenge this season."

Alex was surprised by the request, but he trusted David's instincts. David studied his opponents well before his team met them on the field.

"Who else should come along?" Alex asked.

David shook his head. "Handle it yourself. I have plans for the others." He clapped his hand on Alex's shoulder. "Keep up the good work, Alex. Your team shows a lot of talent."

As Alex watched David leave, his brain started to shift gears towards scouting a different team. He hadn't scouted over at Alamo Stadium in two years. He remembered that after the game, he had joined the other coaches down at the Rivercenter Mall for food and drinks. Like many other San Antonians, he took the historic river area for granted and rarely went down there.

It was then Alex allowed himself to smile. Any woman who would sit through a freshman football game ought to be treated to a nice dinner and a ride on a riverboat.

Chapter Three

The whirring motors of the square river barge, its deck lined with colored benches for people to easily view the river sights, set the pace for the autumn Saturday afternoon. Slowly, the driver steered from its dock on the lowest level of the three-story Rivercenter Mall, and into the steady flow of the San Antonio River.

If anyone had told Kaylene she'd spend the rest of the day holding Alex's hand and riding on a river barge, she wouldn't have believed it. Yet, here she was, and beside her sat a good-looking Texan in jeans and a plaid western shirt who barely resembled the man she had seen on the football field four hours ago.

Alex's invitation to keep him company tonight had caught her by surprise. Her enthusiastic "I'd love to" startled her even more. She didn't like football, yet she agreed to attend two games the same day. Was she crazy?

In the car, Kaylene's nervous energy had kept the conversation on trivial matters. She hadn't known how to talk to a coach about losing his first game.

On the Riverwalk, as they waited for the next boat to stop, Alex had mentioned the game himself. As he had spoken about the positive aspects of the game and dismissed the loss as more luck than skill, Kaylene had seen a coach who didn't dwell on the down side of losing. As Alex discussed his football players, she saw how much he cared about the boys' feelings. It was then she knew that Alex didn't have self-serving motives for asking Mrs. Dunn to change the report deadline. Kaylene admired Alex's attention to academics too, because she noticed yesterday that every boy wearing a football jersey had turned in a book report.

"So Alex, do you have a different strategy for next week's game?" she asked with interest. She enjoyed listening to him talk about his team.

"I have a few tricks I might try," Alex answered with a touch of a grin on his face. He settled back against the railing.

"Tell me about your tricks, Coach." She teased him with a smile, ready to play along with his mood.

"I'll probably try Felix as wide receiver, maybe give Sam a shot at middle linebacker, and try Raymond out as a nose guard. I'll keep Ralph next to Bobby, though, because together they're a tough defense. Central had a lot of trouble getting past my line."

Kaylene was lost in the football jargon. She looked at Alex apologetically. "I'm sorry I asked. I wouldn't know one football player from another except that they wear different numbers."

"So ask me a question," he responded casually. "What don't you understand?"

Kaylene hesitated. She hated to reveal her ignorance. She didn't really care about football, but she did care about Alex. His unexpected invitation showed her that he valued her companionship. And didn't a friend try to learn more about something important to the other?

"What if I begin by telling you about the positions I just mentioned?" Alex asked her in a gentle voice. Once he began talking, she responded with her own questions. His explanations were carefully worded in terms she could understand.

By the time they returned to the lagoon, Kaylene knew she could watch a game and understand something besides touchdowns and penalty flags. She had also learned that Alex was a good teacher for beginners.

She accepted Alex's assistance out of the boat, then stood close to him on the narrow brick walkway. Their eyes met briefly, and he smiled. He slipped his arm around her waist and gently led her towards the mall.

As they passed the umbrella-covered tables on the patio area surrounding the river lagoon, Kaylene raised her eyes to admire the three-story glass structure, which allowed patrons to view the river from all angles. The buildings were connected by covered walkways, and each floor by outdoor stairs, inside elevators, and escalators.

She stopped abruptly, pushing against Alex's hard chest when a little boy raced directly in front of her, poking her with his pointy elbow and running over her toes. She barely saw the black hair as he zoomed past them heading towards the edge of mossy green river. She guessed he couldn't be more than five.

"Mama! *¡Mira al pescadito!*" he cried, pointing one pudgy brown finger towards the minnows swimming close to the water's surface.

"Alfredo! *¡Cuidado!*" The worried scream came from behind them, and it startled the boy, who teetered close to the edge.

Kaylene felt Alex release her, and in two quick steps, he grabbed the toppling boy by the back of his yellow T-shirt. In a fluid motion, he lifted the boy into his arms and stared into the rounded, black eyes.

"You okay, *amigo*?" Alex's voice was very calm and gentle.

The boy nodded, although Kaylene noticed his trembling bottom lip.

"*Gracias, Señor. Gracias. Muchas gracias.*" A thin woman, whose face resembled the little one looking at Alex, had appeared and poured forth her thanks. She stretched out her arms to the boy, and he quickly leaned towards her. "*Gracias, Señor.*"

"You're very welcome," Alex said softly, as he released the boy to his mother.

The woman nodded at Kaylene and took her son away.

Kaylene wrapped her hands around Alex's arm, feeling the strong muscles beneath his shirt. "I guess you're a hero."

He shrugged. "I'm just glad I didn't have to jump in after him." He chuckled, and looked down at her. "I don't think you'd like me smelling like an old river the rest of the night."

Kaylene gently stroked his cheek. "It would have been for a good cause. I wouldn't mind." She saw his eyes sparkle and wondered how everything could feel so natural when she hadn't seen this man in ten years. No one made her feel like Alex did.

"If we don't eat soon, I may be late for the game." Alex's voice pulled her back into reality. He had to scout a game. That was his priority tonight.

Kaylene nodded slowly. "Yes, Alex. Let's go inside and eat."

After a pleasant dinner, Alex drove to Alamo Stadium, a big athletic complex surrounded Brackenridge Park, Trinity University, and the McAllister Freeway. They entered through a special gate after Alex showed the man a card in his wallet. Holding Alex's binocular case, Kaylene followed him up cement steps into a section off to the side of the press box specifically for football scouts. She felt awkward because she was the only female in the box, and even when Alex introduced her to coaches he knew, still felt like an alien in a different world.

As Alex began watching the game and taking notes on his clipboard, Kaylene felt she shouldn't bother him with questions about a sport she cared for only because it was important to him. As she watched him drawing lines on papers marked with X's and O's as plays progressed, she marveled again at the seriousness of high school football. What ever happened to playing on a team because it was fun?

As if Alex was reading her mind, he suddenly said, "You want every advantage over your opponent, Kaylene. A scouting report can explain a weakness you might exploit, or pin-point a key player who might require special handling."

He probably noticed her watching the band and pep squads more than the teams because at half-time he said, "I know this isn't very exciting for you, Kaylene, but I'm glad you came with me tonight." He gently pressed his shoulder against hers.

His words lighted a hopeful candle inside her. She closed her eyes, wishing for more moments of undivided attention.

Then the game resumed, and his professional manner locked her out of his thoughts completely. She disliked feeling lonely among hundreds of people. Even after Alex's considerate explanations, she discovered going to football games could never replace other activities people shared. She liked to go to movies, go bowling, or walk downtown by the river. A football game wasn't conducive to romance. She pasted on a smile when Alex glanced at her, but inside, she was frowning.

—∞—

Crossing his arms over the steering wheel, Alex looked out the front windshield. "If you don't mind, we'll sit here and let traffic ease up. There's only one exit out of this stadium, and too many impatient drivers." He glanced her way.

He saw Kaylene wiggle her hips into the bench seat of the car, then stretched her shoulders from side to side with a tiny moan. She pressed herself against the pillowed head rest, closing her eyes.

"Are you tired?" he asked, hoping the night hadn't bored her so much that she was ready to ditch Alex the coach as fast as possible.

"I'm just a little stiff. Not used to bleachers, I guess."

"I give a great massage," Alex purred.

A slight smile curved her lips. "I just bet you do. Thanks, anyway."

Alex's sly chuckle made her open her eyes. Softly laughing, she raised her head. With her fingers, she gathered her dark hair in a pony tail, then shook it over her shoulders.

He reached out to smooth the silken strands, allowing himself the pleasure of touching her. Instinctively, his hand moved to stroke her cheek, then slide along the gentle curves of her face.

Her large, dark brown eyes raised to his. Framed by long, black lashes, they reminded him of rich chocolate. He bridged the short gap by leaning towards her as he smoothly captured her shoulders, pulling her towards him.

She trembled when his lips touched hers. She parted her lips to receive his next kiss, circling his neck with her hands. She tasted of cola and popcorn, her skin was softly scented. He released her lips to hold her against him. Alex tried to pretend he wasn't sitting in a football stadium parking lot with his scouting report tossed in the back seat.

A loud car horn broke the moment, as reality crashed in on him. Asking Kaylene to attend games he scouted was impractical for him and unfair to her. He could hardly concentrate because the winds carried her perfume in his direction, making him forget which player carried the ball. And he knew, by her quiet manner, she was bored by the game.

Slowly, he released her and straightened up. He looked away and started the car, unable to give her answers for the questions burning in her eyes.

—∿∿—

Kaylene looked out the car window, but she didn't see much beyond the outlines of trees and homes in the dark neighborhoods. She felt unable to say much to Alex after his kiss. Her heart had only seconds ago begun to beat a more natural rhythm. She needed to explore her feelings for Alex carefully. She didn't want to get caught in something that was one-sided. She did that once her first year in college, and knew it wasn't worth the humiliation.

She glanced at Alex, tapping his fingers on the steering wheel to the beat of a George Strait song. Alex had always been honest with her in the past. She had no reason to believe he would change.

"I had a good time tonight, Alex."

"Great! I had fun too." He smiled quickly in her direction, then returned his eyes to the road in front of him.

"Any chance we can do this again?" She usually wasn't so direct with a man she dated, but she wanted to know if he thought the relationship was worth his time.

He laughed. "I seem to eat, sleep, and breathe football. Who in their right mind does that?"

If he was trying to avoid her question with a joke, she didn't think it very funny. She folded her arms across her chest, and glared out the car window.

"Actually, the next few weeks I'll be scouting out of town a lot. Leon Creek plays four small town schools in a row. You'll be too busy doing student teaching to go out much."

Irritation compounded Kaylene's mood. Couldn't he forget about the professional aspects of their lives, and think about something personal between them? Even a phone call now and then between scouting teams?

"I make time for other things besides my work," Kaylene replied in a quiet voice. She glanced at Alex and caught his quick look, but he didn't comment.

They drove in silence until they reached Kaylene's apartment.

Alex stopped the car, turned off the ignition, and sighed as Kaylene unbuckled her seat belt. "Thanks again, Alex."

She felt his hand on her arm, and looked in his direction wishing she could see his face better.

"I loved today, Kaylene. For a while, I could forget I was such a busy coach. But the fact is, I'm very busy. I don't think you understand just how busy I am."

Kaylene felt his hand gently slide over her arm. "Maybe I don't understand all the demands on your time, Alex. But I just feel there ought to be more to life than a person's job." She steadied herself for a Coach Garrison statement about priorities and responsibilities, but he didn't say anything at all.

He leaned forward and kissed her lips softly. When he moved away, and unbuckled his seat belt, she only felt more confused.

He held her hand as they walked to her porch.

"Would you like to come inside a while and talk?" Kaylene asked, turning to him.

Alex stopped on the sidewalk, releasing her hand. "It's late. I need to get home." His eyes looked tired. The rest of his face looked like he had just fumbled a touchdown.

"Well, okay. Good night." Kaylene turned and walked up the steps. She barely heard his "Good-bye," but the rapid steps as he left her apartment echoed in her ears, even after she had gone inside.

She tossed her purse and keys on the coffeetable, feeling sad and confused. She saw her lesson plan book open on the sofa and sighed. Teaching was something she had wanted to do all her life. *Falling in love,* she thought, *would be wonderful too.*

—∞—

"Good morning. I'm Ms. Morales. I'll be teaching you the next two units in grammar and literature."

Kaylene stood before first period, trying to hold the attention of twenty-five students. She knew she looked professional in her navy blue skirt and striped blouse. Her dark hair was pinned up in a twist.

"I'll begin by reassigning your seats. Since I don't know your names, a seating chart will help me get to know you."

Low grumbles and complaints broke the curious silence.

Kaylene had determined that placing students where she wanted them was a starting point to prove who was in charge. She glanced once at Mrs. Dunn, who sat at the rear of the room with an icy stare that challenged students to disobey and face dire consequences.

"I'd like to ask these first two rows of students to stand and move to the back of the room." Once they did, she began to read off the names and students reseated themselves in the next available desk.

She wanted to smile as she accomplished the first task, but restrained herself because she wanted to maintain her no-nonsense appearance. Her young face and delicate stature were two qualities she considered disadvantages to enforcing discipline. A serious mask hid the nervous teacher inside.

Kaylene walked to the teacher's desk, put down her attendance book, and picked up the grammar text. She ignored the slight tremble of her hands, and swallowed the pasty taste in her mouth. On rubbery legs she returned to the imaginary circle she mapped out as the ideal place from which to teach. Then she teetered in her black high heels, which suddenly seemed to pinch her toes.

"We'll begin today with connectives. They are also called conjunctions. Does anyone know why we call them connectives?"

There was silence, a roaring quiet that rocked the classroom and Kaylene with it. Her body swayed slightly, but she forced herself to continue as if someone answered. "Connectives are used to connect two shorter sentences into a longer one. For example, here are two sentences: *John ran into the store. He wanted to buy a loaf of bread.* You could connect these two sentences together with the connective and say: *John ran into the store* because *he wanted to buy a loaf of bread.*" She continued explaining, carefully mentioning each type of connective and five examples.

Kaylene was midway through her notes when she looked at the students. They sat in their desks, books closed, notebooks unopened, watching her with a variety of expressions. She wondered why they hadn't written down everything she said.

Whenever she listened to any of her professors, she always took precise notes. Didn't these students understand the importance of her lecture?

Then it hit her. *High school freshmen didn't take notes.* They probably didn't know they were supposed to. She never told them: This is important. Write it down.

Kaylene cleared her throat, feeling perspiration on her forehead. "If you would open your notebooks, I'll begin putting the lists of connectives on the board. I would like you to copy them in your notebook."

A hand shot up.

Kaylene looked at the face, them fumbled with the seating chart and her texbook. She had to look from the blonde boy to her chart twice before she decided who he was. "Yes, Mark?"

"I don't have my notebook. Can I get it from my locker?"

He shrugged and grinned sheepishly. "Sorry. I didn't think we would need it today." Kaylene glanced at Mrs. Dunn, but her face was a blank stare. The decision was Kaylene's. "You can go, Mark." Then she wondered if she should continue with one student out of the room.

Two other hands shot up.

She frowned trying to place faces with names on the chart.

"I don't have anything to write with, Miss."

"Can I use looseleaf? I don't have a notebook."

Kaylene gave one girl her pencil and told the other not to lose her paper because she would need her notes to study for a test.

Kaylene placed her book on the desk, picked up the small note card on which she had written connectives, and went to the board. She picked up a long piece of chalk and as she placed the point against the blackboard, it snapped in two, one piece popping back into her face.

Kaylene hopped back, her feet sliding. She grabbed the chalk ledge to steady herself.

She ignored the snickers, giggles, and comments, and in a loud voice said, "The first type of connectives are *coordinating connectives.*" She wrote in big print on the board with the half-piece of chalk.

The period ticked by before she knew it. She couldn't give the next list until they copied the first. Some students worked very slowly, leaving gaps in her lecture. The awkward situation made her uncomfortable, especially when those who wrote quickly started conversing with their friends. She expected students to wait patiently in silence. What would Mrs. Dunn think of the constant buzz of teenage whispers in her classroom?

With only two minutes remaining, and one more list to go, Kaylene realized she hadn't reached her daily goal. She'd have to revise her lesson plans. She thought she had prepared so carefully yesterday afternoon.

Then Mark, the boy who had left earlier in the period, walked into the classroom.

41

Kaylene tensed. "Where have you been?"

He tossed his book from hand to hand.

"I went to get my notebook," he said calmly.

"You left twenty minutes ago,"she replied.

"My locker is in another building." His green eyes shone with his private joke.

Each giggle she heard added to her anger. She gave the boy a stare that could melt an iceberg. "Find a friend and copy his notes. You'll need them tomorrow."

The boy shrugged unconcernedly and returned to his desk.

—⁓—

A loud knock interrupted fifth period's lecture.

Kaylene sighed and walked to the door.

A small, pudgy woman stood there. "Are you Mrs. Dunn?"

"No. I'm Ms. Morales, her student teacher."

"I'm from the attendance office. We didn't get an attendance sheet from you last period."

"I sent one. There were no absences in my fourth period class."

"There were three freshmen absent from the other periods on their schedule, but you listed them as present in your class. They didn't report to their fifth-period class. Were they actually here, or did you make a mistake?" Her nasal whine was amplified in the quiet classroom.

Kaylene tried to keep her impatience out of her voice. "I called the roll, and someone said 'Here' each time. I assumed they were in class."

"Well, they weren't. They're on absentee slips from four other teachers."

The temperature in the room went up ten degrees as Kaylene looked down at the little woman with the confident sneer. She despised the woman for humiliating her in front of the class whose respect she was working so hard to obtain.

"I'm sorry. I'll be more careful in the future."

The woman nodded and walked out of the room as fast as her fat little feet would take her.

Kaylene turned back to the students who watched her curiously. Under other circumstances, Kaylene would have made a silly comment to ease the situation. The laughter would break the tension, and she could easily get back to her lectures. She couldn't do that now. She would lose control and teaching was serious business.

Kaylene squared her shoulders, and precisely guided her steps back to the board. She wrote down the next connective.

Chapter Four

Kaylene answered the doorbell of her apartment after the first ring. The uniformed delivery man carried an arrangement of scarlet roses set against a fan of leaves in a white vase. The romantic fragrance lifted her beyond the long, harrowing day she had experienced into the gentle world of beauty and love.

Kaylene smiled at the man, and closed the door. Placing her bouquet on the maple coffee table in front of her blue plaid sofa, she opened the card.

> *GOOD LUCK STUDENT TEACHING.*
> *NO DAY IS EVER AS BAD AS THE FIRST ONE.*
> *ALEX*

Kaylene leaned down to capture the fragrance deep inside her. His sentimental gesture was surprising. *Why would he do this,* she wondered, *when our parting Saturday night had been so lukewarm?*

She moved the roses to the kitchen table, where she worked on her lesson plans. Her mind often wandered off connectives as she stared at the roses and contemplated Alex's sensitivity to her insecure feelings after her first day as a high school teacher. She yearned to thank him for his gift, and debated whether she should call him.

Finally, close to 9 p.m. she dialed information, then Alex's number. Twisting the phone cord through her fingers, she listened to the rings.

"Hello!" He sounded as if he had run to the phone.

"Hello, Alex. It's Kaylene."

"Hi!" He expelled his breath slowly. "I heard the phone ringing from outside. I just got home."

"I won't keep you but a second. I just wanted to thank you for the roses. They're lovely." She smiled brightly, even if he couldn't see it.

"I hope the first day of student teaching wasn't too bad," he replied.

Kaylene laughed, the first time she allowed herself to see humor in the day. "I'm lucky Mrs. Dunn didn't ask for another student teacher."

"She wouldn't do that. I've seen the other student teachers. She has a prize," Alex said, the warmth in his voice consoling her. "So why don't you tell me about your first day."

Suddenly, the day's adventures poured forth.

"I allowed a boy to go to his locker and he never came back. The attendance office said I was the only teacher who marked three students present, when everyone else said they were absent. At lunch, the salt shaker uncapped on my food. And you remember the two girls who were fighting in the hall? They're both in my sixth period. And my seating chart placed them right next to each other. I listened to them insult each other all period."

Alex chuckled, then coughed. "Sorry! I shouldn't laugh."

"It's okay. It sounds funny to me too, now that it's over."

"Just remember, Kaylene. Each day will have a new set of problems, but no day will be like the first." Alex chuckled again. "On my first day in student teaching, I set off the fire alarm in the gym. Three girls convinced me they might be pregnant, and couldn't dress out for P.E. I locked my supervising teacher's keys in the weight room, and almost dropped a five-pound weight on the head coach's foot."

Kaylene laughed at his stories. She stretched her legs in front of her, relaxing for the first time all day. "Alex, your roses helped me get back some confidence. Did someone do the same for you?"

"Actually, a friend gave me a six-pack of beer. I thought you'd enjoy the roses more. So how was the teaching? Did you dazzle them with brilliance?"

She smiled at his teasing. "I don't think so. It took so long for me to write information and erase it. They spent all period copying notes. I wish I had more blackboard space."

"Did anyone whistle when you turned your back on them?"

"Yes, that happened once. I wanted to laugh, but I ignored it."

"Good. If they don't get a reaction, they usually don't make it a habit. You know, Kaylene, if you don't want to erase so much, write your notes on a transparency and project them on an overhead projector," Alex suggested.

"I thought about it, but when I went to the Audio-Visual Lab, there wasn't one available until Friday." She shrugged off the frustration. "I decided that I would type up copies of what I put on the board today, and give them out later. Maybe two copies will make them study more." Enjoying the friendly conversation, she found a way to continue it. "So, how was your day, Alex?"

"Not bad for a Monday. The usual kids didn't want to dress out for P.E., and I switched some of my players around at practice."

"Do you think it'll make a difference?"

"I hope so. My boys work hard. I'd love to see them win this weekend against Memorial." He paused. "It'll be at the same time and at the same place if you want to come."

47

He reminded her of a child too shy to ask for something he really wanted.

In her most encouraging voice, she said, "I'd love to come to the next game, Alex."

They talked for an hour, and Kaylene realized she treasured the conversation as much as the flowers. He made her laugh, allowed her to share her fears, ideas, and plans, and listened to him discuss football strategy. Even if she didn't understand, she enjoyed his spirited viewpoints. His promise to call her again was as wonderful as his roses.

After her first week study-teaching, the only thing that kept Kaylene from thinking she was crazy for wanting to teach high school were the sight of the roses when she came home, and Alex's phone calls every other night, which enabled her to regain her sense of humor, something she stifled in the name of discipline.

Each period of the day started in chaos. Students always said they had forgotten where they were supposed to sit, and Kaylene lost precious time reseating the students according to her chart.

She lost numerous pencils and pens to students who forgot theirs, borrowed hers, and failed to return them. When she asked students to write a two-page autobiography so she could get better acquainted with them, half the students didn't do the assignment.

Mrs. Dunn told Kaylene she took too much time explaining lessons, and reminded her the connectives unit had to be completed before six weeks' exams, so Kaylene had to leave out some of the exercises she spent hours to create.

Kaylene wanted to heave a gigantic sigh when Friday's last class ended. She'd have two days to recover before she began her frustrating job all over again.

—◆—

Alex's freshman team struggled through their second game. Disappointed when the changes he had made on the line didn't have immediate results, his frustrations shaped his half-time speech into direct orders to concentrate more, and get the plays right.

In the second half, Ralph Hernandez, his tall outside line-backer, intercepted a ball, then ran it back for a touchdown. The team cheered louder after Franklin, the kicker, sent the football between the goals for an extra point.

After the two-minute warning, Memorial scored a touch-down too. Leon Creek had to stop Memorial from making an extra point.

Alex raised his clenched fist, then crossed it over his other arm as a sign he wanted the outside linebacker to rush the kicker. Hands tightening on his hips, he watched the two teams line up. As soon as the ball moved, Ralph forced him-self through Memorial's offensive players. Using his advantage of height and long arms, he stretched up and managed to block the ball.

Jumping along the sidelines, the boys whooped and hollered. Alex grinned at Domingo, who gave him a thumbs-up sign.

A new fire ignited the offensive players, who managed to gain more yards per down than they had the rest of the game. Alex realized his team found new momentum when they saw themselves as winners.

—∿∿—

Kaylene stepped off the short wooden bleachers behind the Leon Creek gym. Pulling her keys from the back pocket of her jeans, she followed the dozen people, mostly parents and siblings of the freshmen, walking towards the parking lot. Excited by Alex's victory, she wished she could congratulate him, but after walking across the field to shake hands with the

Memorial coach, he joined his team in their lively jog off the field with only a quick wave in her direction.

When Alex called her two hours later, she was reclined on the sofa in her apartment proofreading her first test for mistakes.

"Congratulations! I'm so happy for you, Alex!"

"I'm proud of the boys. Ralph surprised us all, but I knew he could block a kick with those gorilla arms of his. Raymond had a great play during the third quarter, and Bobby's throws were very smooth. We just need to get the receivers in the right spot next week. Nothing like a victory to stir things up. The kids are actually looking forward to practice. They want to keep winning," he said, and then laughed. "Winning feels so good!"

Kaylene laughed happily. "I hope your team keeps winning, Coach."

His voice eased into a calmer tone. "Kaylene, I wonder if you'd like to meet me for an early dinner. I'm scouting Edgewood again tonight, but I don't have to meet the others until seven."

"Would you like to come over here?" Kaylene replied. "I put a roast in the crockpot early this morning. It should be ready by four."

"Sounds great. Can I bring something?"

"No, just yourself." She smiled. She was a rookie in the classroom, but she knew how to prepare a home-cooked meal as good as her mother could.

Once Alex promised to be at her place by four, Kaylene made a mad dash at housecleaning. She straightened, vacuumed and hid the clutter, then managed to set a beautiful table.

By the time her cuckoo clock sang out three times, everything was absolutely perfect. She was on her way for a ten-minute soak in her favorite bubble bath when the phone rang.

"Hello, Kaylene. I'm stuck in the middle of fixing broken equipment. I won't be able to make it for supper."

Kaylene's eyes traveled the clean apartment, her mind picturing the white linen tablecloth, Depression-glass vase with three of Alex's roses, and the china she had unpacked from her cedar hope chest. Everything had transformed her tiny kitchen into a romantic setting for two. Disappointment choked her.

"They need everything for tonight's game. I hope you didn't go to much trouble. Maybe another time, okay?"

She waited to hear regret in his voice, but he merely sounded anxious to get off the phone. "Sure, Alex, another time."

"Great. Thanks for understanding. Bye, Kaylene."

She wondered if he even heard her quiet, "Good-bye, Alex," since the phone clicked so quickly. She clapped the receiver down on the telephone. "Yes, Alex! I went through a lot of trouble. I thought you might enjoy something besides restaurant food for a change!" She stomped over to Tempest.

"'I have to fix football equipment.' No one ever gave me *that* line before." She waved a finger at her canary. "Next time he calls, I'll tell him, 'Sorry, Alex, I have my Shakespeare to read.' Let's see if he likes to—" she searched for the right simile— "to feel like a second-string player sitting the bench all season."

The yellow bird chirped and bobbed its head from side to side as if it shared her disapproval of Alex's behavior.

Kaylene sighed unhappily, her fingers winding through the wire cage. "Oh, Tempest! He warned me coaches were busy and it would be a challenge to find time together. And I didn't take him seriously." Leaning her forehead against the cage, she wondered if second-string players ever got a chance to score a touchdown.

When the telephone rang the following afternoon, Kaylene paused at the door wondering if she should ignore it, or answer and be a few minutes late. She decided to risk a frown from her friends.

"Hi, Kaylene. Are you busy?"

Alex's voice stirred up emotions she wanted to bury. She was glad he called, yet still felt angry about yesterday.

"Actually, Alex, I'm on my way out."

"Oh, I thought we might get together and do something fun."

"I'm on my way to do something fun." She wanted to show him that her world didn't revolve around this unpredictable relationship. She had other options besides waiting for him to call when his schedule permitted.

"Kaylene, I'm very sorry about yesterday. My head coach walked in right after we made plans, and told me about the broken equipment. Freshman coaches usually get the dirty jobs." He cleared his throat. "I called you at half-time hoping we could meet later, but you were gone."

"I went out." Not one to drown in self-pity, Kaylene had gone to the University Student Center to listen to the band that played there on Saturday nights. She had run into a group of graduate students, and remained there the rest of the evening.

"Well, I won't keep you." An exhausted sigh followed his statement. "I'll call you again, okay?"

Kaylene squeezed the telephone receiver tightly. She really wanted to be with Alex, not a group of casual friends. Last night, she wondered what it would be like to do something with him completely separate from football. "Would you like to join my friends and me? We're going miniature golfing."

An easy chuckle traveled the phone line. "I haven't done that since high school. Considering I've been indoors watching football films for six hours, a game of golf sounds wonderful. Where shall I meet you?"

—∞—

"Ugh!" Kaylene stomped her sneaker against the green turf of the miniature golf course. She had missed the hole by a fraction of an inch. Twisting the club handle, she stepped up on the curb, leaned against a big mesquite tree to await her next try, and enjoyed the scenery.

She always thought of this old miniature golf course as a combination of tropics and Texas. Between different courses, banana trees with long, green leaves flapped in the breeze. Green stalks with big purple leaves, shaped like the ears of an elephant, seemed to grow wild. Planted alongside were mountain laurel trees wtih black skinny trunks and hard red beans among the leaves. All sizes of shrubs and agarita plants with their tiny three-sided pointed leaves lined the fence. There was enough variety in the landscape and plenty of diverse challenges on the course to suit everyone.

Kaylene smiled as Alex stood in profile on the final hole of the first course, both his hands gripping the short club. Dressed casually in worn denims and a white T-shirt decorated with a burnt-orange Longhorn, he looked relaxed in contrast to the tight expression of concentration on his face. Carefully, his eyes gauged the distance from his ball to the hole, then hit it forward. His ball rolled slowly, but missed the green cup too.

A quick laugh burst from Kaylene.

Chuckling, he swung the club over his shoulder and walked towards her. "This one may be a tie breaker. Your turn, Kaylene," he said, coming to stand beside her.

Kaylene nodded, feeling her face grow warm as he studied her. She started to move away, but he grabbed her elbow and pulled her close. Before she knew it, his lips captured hers in a gentle kiss. He smiled as she blinked at him.

"Just a kiss for luck. You make this shot, and you win the game." His voice seemed nonchalant, but his eyes shone with an intensity that had nothing to do with golf.

"If I make this shot, I get another kiss." Kaylene's demand was out of her mouth quickly. If she didn't make the most of the time they had together, she felt he'd be off to do something or other for a football team.

She moved away to her ball nestled next to Alex's in a slight incline. She tried to keep her mind focused as she positioned herself over her red ball. She lowered her gold club beside it, and bent over to study the situation. She wanted another kiss. Her eyes traveled the distance three times before she was ready to swing.

Alex's hand abruptly clamped down on her arm. "Don't move!" His quiet command startled her, but she remained still.

"What's wrong?" she whispered. What this some dramatic ploy so she wouldn't win the game?

"There's a wasp on you. Don't move."

"A wasp? Where?" Immediately her eyes darted over her yellow blouse and white jeans.

Then, she felt Alex's hand brush her backside, and he quickly pushed her away. The gold club flew out of her grip.

Kaylene spun around to see the wasp flying off into the bushes lining the fence.

"I thought you were trying to keep me from winning the game," Kaylene said, placing a hand on her buzzing heart. She looked into Alex's face gratefully. "Thanks."

Alex wrapped his arm around her shoulder. "If you wouldn't let me massage you last week, I knew you weren't going to let me administer first aid for a bee sting."

Kaylene fluttered her eyes. "How noble of you."

"Actually, I'm very selfish." His tone changed completely. "I called when I returned from Kerrville, and there was no answer. Were you with someone special last night?"

The question was so unexpected Kaylene's lips popped apart. She wondered if her vivid imagination shaded his eyes a deeper shade of green or they truly sparkled with jealousy.

"I never asked if there was someone else, and I—" Alex paused, choosing his words carefully. "I just wondered."

Kaylene stroked his jaw. The shadow of his beard reminded her of fine sandpaper. "I went out with friends, Alex. A group of graduate students. You didn't expect me to stay home because you canceled our dinner, did you?"

His hand wrapped in her dark hair, as his eyes scanned her face. "Actually, I'm glad you have other friends to be with. I just wondered if I had some competition I should worry about."

She lowered her eyes. "No, Alex, there's no one special." A sadness tugged at her. Alex didn't need to worry about other men competing with him, but *she* felt a deep competition— with a hard-hearted wench she called football.

"Shall we finish this game and tell the others good-bye so I can take you to dinner?" His lips brushed the top of her head.

She rested against him. She felt selfish and wanted all his attention for herself. "I can reheat the roast if you don't mind leftovers."

"That would be fine. Stay here." Alex let her go. He bent over, scooping the two golf balls into his hand. He dropped them both into the hole, the one leading to the chute in the office. He carried their clubs in one hand, holding hers in the other as they found her friends on the second course.

After a polite good-bye, and ignoring the suggestive grins from her girlfriends, Kaylene and Alex walked back to her car. She unlocked the door, and he opened it for her.

Before she could step in, Alex slipped his arms around her waist and pulled her to him.

"The game ended in a tie. I still get my kiss." He bent down and gently pressed his lips against hers.

Kaylene's hands tugged him closer, continuing the kiss for a long, satisfying moment. She felt light-headed and giddy when she released him. "Since it was a tie, I thought I'd get my kiss too."

Alex smiled. "Any time, my lady. Any time."

———∞∞———

"I cook on weekends and eat leftovers all week," Kaylene explained as she rinsed an enamel dish under the faucet.

Alex wiped a plate dry and stacked it in the wooden cupboard above him. "I'll remember that. Maybe I can manuever another invitation between games on Saturday or after work on Sunday."

"Well, if you eat as much as you did today, I won't have much left for leftovers." She teased him, although his appetite and compliments warmed her heart's most feminine places. She enjoyed cooking, but some of the men she had dated believed an expensive dinner at an exclusive restaurant was more impressive. Others were so accustomed to fast food they preferred only hamburgers or pizza before making a fast move on her.

Alex seemed more concerned about taking their relationship one step at a time, and that suited her just fine. So did the ordinary aspects of a relationship like laughing together, doing the dishes, and talking about goals and aspirations.

"I should barbecue for you sometime," Alex said, taking the dish from her and drying it. "But don't expect dinner from me until after football season, okay?"

She turned off the faucet and dried her hands on a towel hanging from a wire rack above the kitchen sink. "I'm learning that no plans of any kind should be made during football season."

"Flexibility helps a lot. I do more of the dirty jobs as a freshman coach. Fix equipment, wash uniforms, write scouting reports. As I move up into the varsity level, my job will change. Less scouting, but more pressures to win."

"Would you like to be the head coach some day?"

Alex placed the pot on the counter, tossing the towel inside. He looked at Kaylene as he contemplated her question. "I'd like to stay in a small place like Leon Creek where the head coach is also athletic director. I like to give orders. But you know that, don't you?" He winked at her and she laughed.

Alex took her hand and led her to the living room. "And you, Miss Kaylene? What are your plans?"

"To survive student teaching!"

She settled on the sofa, curling her legs beneath her.

Alex sat down, stretching his arm behind her. His hand gently rubbed her shoulder.

"I hope to grab a spot in mid-semester at a high school. Someone from Jefferson contacted my professor just this week about an English position opening in January." She tilted her head to rest it against his arm. "Would you mind if I found a job at Leon Creek?" She glanced at him.

"I'd really mind if you moved with your parents to Laredo," he replied, then curled his arm around her shoulders.

"I won't go to Laredo, Alex."

When Alex kissed her slowly, she treasured each second of pleasure. The lingering effect sent echoes into the caverns of her soul, a place no kiss ever reached before.

Her fingers wandered through the soft waves of his light brown hair, then trailed the contours of his face. Each texture she explored, she found contrast; just like the man himself.

She couldn't predict where the relationship with this coach would take her. No education textbook she ever read had a chapter on someone like Alex. Luckily, as an English major, she had read her fill of love sonnets and daring romances; maybe that would help.

Alex whispered her name, before he kissed her again.

And then again, maybe not.

Chapter Five

Hands popped up before Kaylene finished giving out the tests. She sighed. *Now what? How did freshmen come up with so many questions?*

She returned to her desk, picked up the seating chart, trying to connect names of the students who needed assistance.

"Ms. Morales, I don't understand the directions," said the boy in the last desk of the first row.

Impatience twisted her nerves. "What don't you understand, Felix?"

"The directions, Ms. Morales. What do they mean?"

Kaylene studied Felix's pale face. His confusion looked genuine.

She picked up a copy of the test. "Supply an appropriate connective for each pair of sentences below. Make each pair of simple sentences into a compound sentence." She looked at Felix. "The directions are clear to me."

He persisted. "I don't understand the directions, Miss."

She devised another explanation. "You need to write down a connective that will connect the two shorter sentences into one longer one."

A hand caught her attention because it waved so urgently.

Not even bothering with the seating chart, she nodded to the girl. "Yes? What's wrong?"

"Miss, I left my connective list at home," the blonde said. "I don't have a list to use for the test."

Kaylene frowned. "You don't need a list. This is a test. You were supposed to memorize the list of connectives. I told you that Friday."

Then she noticed the whispers between two girls in the center of the room. She started down the aisle between them, and they quickly bowed their heads over their test papers.

In a loud, firm, voice, Kaylene announced, "There will be no more questions. Do the best you can. No talking of any kind." She returned to the front of the class room to monitor the test.

There was silence until some students finished their tests within ten minutes. She had planned for the test to take the students the entire period and didn't prepare anything else for the class. She quickly realized that ninth grade students weren't resourceful with unoccupied time. She spent the rest of the period demanding silence when they wanted to talk to their friends who had finished their tests too.

But Kaylene learned from the experience, and when second period entered the room, she took five minutes before distributing the test to write out the directions on the board, explain what she wanted, and give examples. She created a writing assignment for the students after the test. After second period ended, her head ached from the stress.

At fourth period, Kaylene noticed Ralph's proud strut into the room. He smiled at Kaylene, a dazzling display of white teeth she assumed was meant to charm her. Or maybe to remind her that he was an important football player now.

Kaylene wanted to tell him she was proud of his playing, but worried her friendliness might be misunderstood. She needed to keep her distance from the students to maintain her authority. She folded her arms across her, her face impassive. "Good morning, Ralph."

He stopped to acknowledge her greeting. He nodded. "Hey, Miz Morales. Have a good weekend?"

Kaylene forced Alex's handsome face from her thoughts. This wasn't the time to remember yesterday's special moments.

Ralph's black eyes gleamed over her. His look wasn't insulting, but it made Kaylene step back nonetheless. "I saw you at Cool Crest yesterday," he stated.

Kaylene's body stiffened when he mentioned the golf course. Did he see Alex swat the wasp off her hips, or the two kisses in the parking lot because their score tied? Her private life was the last thing she wanted to discuss with one of her students. She had to pretend indifference as she gave him a calm look. She shrugged and replied, "I hope you had a good time."

Ralph raised one eyebrow. "I think you had a better time than I did. I just played golf." His thick lips thinned, as his black eyes penetrated her thoughts.

Kaylene's heart pounded in her ears waiting for the boy to mention Alex. What would the athlete say to her now that he knew she dated his coach?

A deep, throaty chuckle was Ralph's final parting as he resumed his proud gait towards his assigned desk near the windows.

Throughout the class, Ralph seemed intent on watching her and seemed to enjoy it when their eyes locked. He would wink twice, and smile knowingly. With a definite shake of his head, he returned his attention to his work.

His antics unnerved her, but she kept her feelings submerged until the period bell rang. Ralph left her room, whistling under his breath. She rubbed her forehead as she wondered if Ralph planned to tell everyone about his discovery.

61

The nerve-wracking day didn't improve when Mrs. Dunn discussed Kaylene's first test after school.

"You shouldn't have to take the time to explain directions," Mrs. Dunn remarked, shaking her head as she studied Kaylene's first attempt to create a freshman exam. "You need to write directions students understand. You think like a college student, not like a freshman. You realize you'll have to throw away this test and give them another."

Kaylene nodded. She felt like an ignorant freshman as she faced Mrs. Dunn across the desk. "I decided since so many failed it, I'd give them another test Wednesday."

"Keep in mind, next Friday is six weeks' exams. We can't afford to give any more second tests. I want to see your part of the six weeks' test by Tuesday, Kaylene. If you need to rewrite it, I can tell you then. I don't want to have to stand in line Friday morning at the copy machine, you know." She let the test sheet fall to the desk, then began to retrieve her purse and briefcase. "After Wednesday, I'll be in and out. Are you ready to handle the students alone?"

Do I have a choice? Kaylene swallowed the dryness of panic. "I'll be fine."

"As long as you don't make idle threats, you shouldn't have problems. The kids know better than the teacher what you can and can't do. Don't let the boys bully you, either."

Kaylene raised an eyebrow. Was that permission to bring a baseball bat to class?

When she proposed such a crazy plan that night on the telephone to Alex, he laughed.

"I know how you feel, but you can't do that! You could knock out one of my athletes. They need to play ball for me, okay?" His voice changed into the soothing, warm tone Kaylene loved most. "Everything will be fine. As long as you keep them busy, they won't have time to cause trouble."

Kaylene doubted Alex's wisdom as her patience thinned at the noisy, uncooperative spirit in Thursday's fourth period.

She couldn't sit behind her desk and help students because every time she gave someone her attention, the noise level increased.

Kaylene checked her work sheet without losing her temper, but as she began her next lecture on the final type of connectives, Ralph's constant whispers became a nuisance. She waited silently, her body rigid.

Ralph caught her fierce glare. He smiled and waved at her. The two boys beside him snickered.

Three different times Kaylene had to stop her lecture, refusing to compete with Ralph and his friends. Finally, she addressed the problem directly. "Ralph, Pete, and Adam, I intend to teach what I have planned for today, even if it means going into the lunch period."

Ralph's eyes narrowed as he clamped his lips together. Kaylene guessed he was debating whether or not to call her bluff. She hoped he wouldn't try it. She was hungry, and didn't want to talk through her lunch time.

She explained an adverbial clause and answered questions non-stop. As she prepared to complete her lecture, Ralph and his friends started socializing again. Kaylene stopped talking, and stood where she was, staring at the clock.

For one century-long minute, she ignored the shuffling, soft coughs, and quick whispers.

She glanced over to see Ralph doodling on his paper.

Kaylene stepped forward and began to talk as if nothing out of the ordinary had happened. She continued talking and writing a few notes on the board and instructed them to copy them.

The bell rang, and everyone started to close their books.

"Wait a minute!" Kaylene's command stalled their departure. "We are not finished yet. There are three more things I have to write on the board. Before you leave, you need to copy them down."

Despite the muffled curses and embarrassed squirming as other students passed in the halls and snickered, Kaylene continued until she finished. Then she looked at the sea of angry faces and quietly said, "You can go now. See you tomorrow."

She looked at the clock. They were only two minutes late for lunch, but it felt like two years had just been wiped away.

The next day, Kaylene realized yesterday's lesson had little effect on Ralph. He started his conversation later in the period, determined to push Kaylene's endurance to the limit.

Finally, she stopped and once again resumed her fixed position as a clock watcher.

One of the athletes in the middle of the room turned around to Ralph's corner. "Will you guys shut up?"

Ralph's obscene answer startled Kaylene. She saw him emphasize his response with a hand gesture. Then he glared at her, his piercing stare a combination of challenge and anger.

Instincts warned her a direct challenge would only provoke Ralph further, so she ignored his behavior for the present. Taking a deep breath, she continued her lecture as if nothing happened. Glancing once at Ralph, she noticed he sat with his arms folded refusing to do any work.

As the bell rang, she moved by the windows. "Ralph, I'd like for you to stay after class a moment. We need to talk." She moved back to her desk, and nodded without smiling at a girl's friendly good-bye.

Ralph slipped his pencil behind his ear. Slouching down, he crossed his arms and waited, a sneer twisting his lips.

Kaylene calmly arranged her papers and stacked books as she waited for the room to empty.

She put a collection of papers she needed to grade into her leather portfolio. She decided to be honest with Ralph, since threats would only back her into a corner. Her voice was very calm. "Would you like to know what I think is the worst thing about teaching? Being a bad guy."

Ralph stared out the window.

"I'm a nice person. I don't like to be the bad guy." She rested her hands on the portfolio. "Don't you ever get tired of being the big, bad jock? You know, people think you are one thing, when you're really someone else? You do what people expect, not what you want."

Ralph looked at her then, his dark eyes narrowing in suspicion.

Since she had his attention, she spoke about the issue keeping them here while others enjoyed lunch. "Ralph, please stop talking in my class. It's very annoying. I'm trying to teach and you are trying to visit. I'm only asking for common courtesy."

His response was a silent black look.

Kaylene's stare challenged his. "And please do not express yourself in such vulgar language either. I don't like it." She put down the portfolio and moved around the desk. "You know, Ralph, I have this theory about cursing. I believe people who can't express themselves intelligently use obscenity as a crutch."

Ralph straightened in his desk, his body rigid. "Are you calling me stupid?"

Kaylene's dark brown eyebrows raised. "If you understood what I just said, Ralph, you are definitely not stupid." She leaned her hips against the desk, clasping her hands at her waist. "I don't think you are a dumb jock, Ralph. Just because you are a football player doesn't mean you can't do other things well. I've seen you play football. You use your size and skill so well. If you'd apply yourself, you'd succeed in school too."

"Football is fun. This stuff is boring and dumb," he told her. "I can play football without knowing connectives."

"No, Ralph, you can't."

As he frowned, she explained. "If you don't do homework, you may not pass my test. Without a passing English grade, you won't play football. So, you lose your fun, but you're still stuck with English class. So, why don't you do me, Coach Garrison, and yourself a favor and work harder in my class?"

His square jaw tensed. "Are you going to tell your boyfriend I'm in trouble in your class?"

Kaylene ignored the implications of his word-choice. Her gaze didn't waver. "What happens in my class is between me and my students. It's no one else's business, even Coach Garrison's." She shrugged. "When you get placed on a list of students who failed a class and can't play ball, Coach Garrison can deal with you." Her hands pressed her growling stomach. "You can go now, Ralph."

He grabbed his books roughly and stalked out.

Kaylene waited until Ralph left, before sighing loudly into the empty classroom. She had said nothing to Alex about Ralph, nothing about his attitude or his behavior. She never told him that the boy knew she and Alex were dating. She wanted to keep her personal relationship with Alex separate from the place where they both worked. It was too special, too wonderful, to get tangled up in the problems they faced as teachers.

—⁓—

The University Student Center gathered a large crowd Saturday night to listen to the country western band.

Alex weaved through the crowded tables searching for Kaylene. He discovered her on the dance floor, tangled among friends doing the Cotton-Eyed-Joe. In the elusive lighting of the room, he saw her eyes twinkle as she hollered to the song. Her slim-fitting blue jeans were speared into calf-length boots. Her legs lifted in two short kicks, then scooted back in the three short steps of the dance. She tossed the mane of dark hair behind her and laughed along with the red-haired woman stumbling along beside her.

As Alex watched Kaylene, he battled the exhaustion from his schedule the last three days. They hadn't spoken since Tuesday, but he remembered her plans to celebrate Linda's birthday, and came straight from the Varsity game hoping to find her. His brain warned him he'd regret the impulsive gesture in the morning, but his heart welcomed the spontaneous burst of joy when Kaylene saw him and waved happily.

Once the lively song ended, a slow ballad began, and Alex swung Kaylene into his arms, settling his hands on her small waist.

"I'm so glad you're here," she said, smiling up at him. Her hands circled his neck as she followed his slow dance steps.

He wanted to tell her how much she meant to him. His recent schedule disrupted the nightly phone calls, and he missed her friendly voice. He couldn't explain the boost he received when he saw her this morning in the bleachers watching his team. Whenever their lives touched in word, action, or thought, he was reminded there was more to life than football, even during football season.

"I feel silly dressed in my coaching shirt, but coming here was a last-minute impulse," Alex told her, unable to voice his deeper feelings.

"I'm getting used to your impulses." She straightened his green shirt collar. One hand slid down his shirt, then fingered the lettering over his pocket. "I feel proud dancing with a member of the Leon Creek Coaching Staff."

"We won tonight. I guess I don't mind wearing it." Actually, the second win for the Varsity would be an item in the sports page tomorrow morning. David Maldonado had broken the losing pattern for Leon Creek, and everyone was optimistic. It was the mood of celebration that had inspired Alex to find Kaylene tonight to share the school's high spirits.

"Everyone loves a winner," she said, her voice a sigh.

Alex pulled her closer, pressing their bodies together. Right now he didn't care about everyone else. Just Kaylene.

—ꟽ—

"Hi, Miz Morales. Did you have a good weekend?"

"My weekend was fine." Kaylene looked up. Ralph's nasty grin made her itch. Had he seen Alex and her at the movies yesterday afternoon? She changed the subject immediately. "Did you study for your test?"

He shook his head. "Too busy this weekend. Just ask Coach Garrison."

She wanted to tell Ralph she had seen his two interceptions and those three quarterback sacks. Why couldn't he put forth half that effort in class? "You might have been busy Saturday. What about Sunday?"

"I'll get by, Miz Morales. You'll see." He leaned his weight into one hip. "I always get by."

His confidence angered her. Did he think she'd pass him because of Alex? Her hands clenched, yet she maintained a quiet voice. "In my class, homework counts for just twenty-five percent. You have only zeros in my grade book. If you didn't prepare for today, you may not get by this time."

One large brown hand wiped away a phony yawn. "*I'm* not worried about it. You don't need to be." He allowed his broad shoulders to lead him around.

Kaylene heard the snickers from three athletes sitting nearby. She gave them a stare that made them stop, and she knew she had perfected "the Dunn look."

The period bell clanged loudly, and Kaylene submerged her emotions behind a mask tight enough to make her teeth ache.

—ꟽ—

Kaylene glanced at the blackboard, then back at her sixth period students. She had repeated her lecture five times and was glad this would be the last time. Her fingers barely touched the cool black surface underneath her two example sentences.

The lion tamer held the nervous beast.
His assistant removed the splinter from his paw.

"Here are a pair of sentences. Can someone give me a connective to join them into one sentence?" Kaylene turned to the class as she repeated the pair of sentences.

"The lion tamer held the nervous breast." Kaylene stammered as embarrassment shot through her. "Uh—I mean nervous beast!"

Her words died in the uproar of laughter. Her cheeks burned like a bad sunburn. How could she have made such a mistake? She could do nothing but surrender helplessly to her sense of humor. She began laughing as well.

"Okay, okay." Kaylene raised her hands, still smiling. "Now that I've provided the joke of the day, let's get back to the sentences on the board."

"I like the sentence you said better than the one on the board," Peter Santos called out.

Kaylene blinked away the last of her embarrassment. "Trust me. You will never see that sentence on a test!" She needed some help to get things back on the right course, so she looked at John Longoria, who was sitting nearby. "John, can you suggest a conjunction to join the two sentences?"

John's brown eyes gleamed mischievously. "Gee, Miss, we didn't think you ever laughed."

Kaylene placed her hand on her hip. "Why, of course I laugh, John. As a matter of fact, I have a pretty good sense of humor."

"Not in this class you don't," he replied, straightening up in his desk. His words held no malice, just honesty. "You never smile or take time to talk to us. You only teach us English."

Kaylene looked around the room as if seeing the students for the first time. John's comment made her aware of the two people she had become: the friendly Kaylene Morales many people loved, and the cold, distant Ms. Morales who was behaving like the teachers Kaylene swore she would never copy.

Slowly she slipped her hands into the side pockets of her red and white striped dress. Curious, friendly faces encouraged her to be relaxed and truthful.

"I'm sorry that I never smile or laugh in class, since I think my sense of humor helps me get through the tough times," Kaylene told them. "I guess I left my ability to laugh at home, and concentrated on my ability to teach instead. That was a mistake. I know you need both to be a good teacher."

A tall girl near the windows raised her hand, and Kaylene nodded to her.

"Ms. Morales, why do you want to be a teacher?" she asked. "They don't make much money."

"I like the idea of working at a job where no two days are ever the same. I enjoy young people, and I love English literature. Put it together, and here I am!"

It suddenly occurred to her that these students knew nothing about her. On the second day of class she expected a two page autobiography from them, but never took time out to discuss herself with them. She remembered her promise to always treat the students the same way she wanted to be treated, and friendly was a better choice than the cold professionalism she had used.

Although she was grateful for her new insights, she knew she had a job to do. "All right—let's get back to connectives. We have our six weeks' test in two days."

Groans and sighs rumbled in the class.

Kaylene went back to the board and asked John for a good conjunction to join the pair of sentences.

After the period ended, Christina and Suzanne asked Kaylene if she liked rock music, and Christina admitted she wanted to be a Spanish teacher. For the first time Kaylene felt comfortable talking to the students after class. She liked the rapport, so different from the distant student-teacher relationship she had maintained in the classroom.

Mrs. Dunn entered the room as Kaylene was laughing with Lori and Lisa Rodriguez about her difficulty in distinguishing the twin sisters.

"We promise not to switch places on you anymore," Lori said, with a grin.

"Well, now that I see you two side by side, I realize Lisa has a dimple on her chin, but you don't." She carefully studied each girl with shoulder length brown hair and blue eyes. "Before my time is over, I'll find other ways to tell you apart."

"See you tomorrow, Ms. Morales," Lisa said. She and Lori smiled at Mrs. Dunn before leaving.

Kaylene drew back her smile as she saw the frown on her supervising teacher.

"Do you think it's wise to be so relaxed with the students?" Mrs. Dunn said, coming to the desk.

Kaylene avoid her ice blue stare by stacking papers. "The school day is over. We all deserve to relax a little."

"Did something happen today? Usually, you and the students race out of here like the place is on fire." Mrs. Dunn lifted a dictionary from the desk and fanned through it. "Is there a problem I should know about?"

"No, no problems." Kaylene met the woman's gaze. Today's sixth period had been the first time she enjoyed herself. She refused to abandon the good feelings. "The kids taught me something about myself today. I've been a phony.

I pretended to be someone I wasn't just so I could maintain control."

"Maintaining control is important, Ms. Morales. If you lose discipline, then how can you teach?"

"I agree, Mrs. Dunn. But I need to find a balance between firm and friendly which suits my personality. I want the kids to respect me, but I also want them to feel comfortable asking me for help. A friendly smile is more encouraging than a scary mask."

"The students might mistake your friendliness as a weakness, Ms. Morales."

Kaylene shook her head. "No, I hope they'll see I'm human and capable of mistakes just like them." A shy smile parted her lips. "I've made dozens of mistakes with you, Mrs. Dunn, and we're still working together."

Mrs. Dunn's serious look was still unbroken. She replaced the dictionary with a firm thud. "If no one made mistakes, then why would we need teachers? Don't be late for the faculty meeting."

Kaylene didn't allow herself the luxury of a private thought until Mrs. Dunn left the room. *How do I satisfy you and still be myself?* One more lesson she needed to learn in the school zone.

Chapter Six

The podium in front of the soda machines was unoccupied when Kaylene entered the cafeteria for the faculty meeting, looking for Mrs. Dunn. She glanced over the teachers chatting among themselves as they sat at the tables.

"I'd ask you to join the coaches, but then, I wouldn't pay attention to the principal."

She blushed as she recognized the voice fanning her ear. She glanced over her shoulder at Alex. Then she remembered they weren't alone.

"Hello, Coach Garrison. Thanks for the invitation, but I want to make sure my supervising teacher gives me an A+. I'll sit by her and take perfect notes."

His words were close to her ear. "Make sure and let me borrow them, Kaylene. I'm bound to snooze through the meeting."

Kaylene turned around to face him. Her eyebrows raised at the gray jogging suit, the jacket zipped midway up his white shirt. "Going running?"

"No." He grinned. "Obviously, you haven't been outside. A cold front blew in this afternoon. It gets chilly on the field." He looked over her striped dress. "Got a sweater?"

Before she could answer, a tall, lanky man arrived behind Alex. A wide grin brightened his brown features. He clapped

Alex on the shoulder. "Is this Mrs. Dunn's student teacher, Alex?"

Kaylene wondered what commentary had been exchanged between the two men as Alex's face seemed to color a slight shade of red.

Dressed in similiar athletic wear, the black-haired stranger extended one of his long arms. "Hello, I'm Domingo Reyes. I coach freshmen too."

She shook his hand. "Hello, I'm Kaylene Morales."

"Are you the reason Alex is in such good humor lately?"

Her eyes shifted back to Alex. He winked.

"Don't look now, Coach, but Lady Dunn is giving us the evil eye." Domingo's ominous tone was filled with sly humor.

Kaylene turned and discovered Mrs. Dunn sitting to their left, her wide face pinched together as she studied them.

Automatically, Kaylene stepped away from Alex and Domingo.

Alex's calm voice soothed her. "There's no rule that says teachers can't talk to coaches, Kaylene."

"Although most teachers hate to talk to coaches on a regular basis," Domingo quipped.

Kaylene suppressed a laugh. She was being overly sensitive, and both men knew it. She did nothing unprofessional talking to Alex, and had no reason to feel embarrassed.

At that moment, a short man with wire glasses entered the cafeteria, and headed toward the podium. The dynamics in the cafeteria subtly changed.

"I'll call you soon, Kaylene," Alex whispered. "See you later."

She nodded, and moved towards Mrs. Dunn's table. She sat down, and quickly opened a notebook.

Mrs. Dunn leaned close to Kaylene's ear. "Have you spoken to Coach Garrison about his football players, Ms. Morales?"

"I don't understand what you mean." She tapped her pencil on the paper as her heart tapped a nervous rhythm inside.

"When I checked the grade book, I noticed six boys who play football are behind in the assignments. Three failed that second test you gave on connectives. Have you told Coach Garrison he may lose part of his team to failing grades?"

Heart pounding, Kaylene stared down at the notebook. "I didn't think about it."

"You should. The book reports were far from perfect, but each athlete turned one in. Ask him to talk to the boys about English or he'll be angry you never warned him about the players' grades."

"Good afternoon, ladies and gentlemen." The principal's booming voice echoed in the building.

Kaylene slowly wrote down the date. She wanted her relationship with Alex to remain on a personal level. She believed she could handle her job alone. She selfishly forgot the boys in her class could affect Alex's success on the field. As a Texas teacher, she knew she'd have to deal with athletes in a "No Pass/No Play" decision. If they failed, by state regulations, they couldn't participate in any extracurricular activity. She just didn't plan on caring about the coach involved when someone failed her class. Here was another situation missing from the education textbooks.

Kaylene forced herself to listen to the principal, and began taking notes just to keep her mind busy. When the meeting ended, she looked around for Alex, but he had already left with the other coaches out a side door.

—∞—

Kaylene sat before the computer staring at a blank screen. If she typed another review sheet with exercises, maybe the information would finally sink in. She leafed through the textbook, frowning at all the boring sentences about people, animals, or places. No one cared about these, especially her freshmen.

What if she created her own sentences? Worksheet sentences that meant something to the students working on them! With a little humor, some wild exaggerations, and a lot of name dropping, maybe she could catch their attention and teach them something at the same time.

Her creative imagination and sense of humor pulled her out of the black mood which had haunted her since the faculty meeting.

She was actually relieved when her cuckoo clock sang out ten times and Alex hadn't called. Mrs. Dunn was right. She and Alex needed to talk about the players, but she'd do it in the professional setting of a classroom, not on the telephone or in her apartment. She'd separate her personal feelings from her professional duties, and hopefully, Alex would do the same.

The next morning, Kaylene altered her usual classroom approach. Instead of waiting at the desk while the students did a work sheet, she circulated the room. She wondered why she had never done this before. It was easier to glance at papers, point out mistakes, and move on. The closeness to the students seemed to relax her. She discovered her presence prohibited conversations among friends too and kept the noise level at a lower volume.

A small hand touched her arm. "Miss, is number seven about me?"

Kaylene concealed her amusement. "I don't know, Maria, is it?"

"No! It's got to be about Maria Cedillo. She's in my second period. This sentence is about her, isn't it?" Bobby asked. He sat in the next row.

"I'm not going to tell." Kaylene moved down the row, smiling, allowing the mystery of name dropping to hold the students' interest as they reviewed connectives.

In fourth period, Ralph raised his eyes and found her watching him. Two fingers motioned to her.

Keeping her face impassive, she walked up to his desk.

A wide smile handsomely altered his features. "Number seventeen is cool, Miss. It's about me, right?"

Kaylene glanced down pretending to read. "Hmmm, I don't know. Are you planning to play in the Super Bowl?"

"I'm big, and I'm good. I bet I could play pro ball!"

Kaylene broached the more important element. "You haven't circled the connective in the sentence yet."

Ralph twirled his pencil. "I'll get to it later."

Kaylene moved behind him. "Maybe we can figure it out together." She leaned over his desk. "There are two sentences in there. Have you figured it out what they are?"

Ralph hunched over his desk. She saw his head move back and forth. "Yeah, I know."

"Well, where's the connective?"

"In the middle. However."

"Great! Do we need any punctuation in that sentence?"

The big shoulders squeezed together. "Maybe." He nodded to himself. "That thing with a period and a comma."

"A semi-colon, Ralph."

"Right."

Kaylene's hand rested gently on his shoulder. "Keep going. You're doing fine."

Ten minutes later, Kaylene was disappointed to see Ralph staring out the window. From her vantage point she saw he stopped working after sentence seventeen. She frowned. Motivating Ralph would take more than one sentence on a work sheet.

She started reviewing the answers to the work sheet and promptly finished as the bell rang. She smiled as she dismissed the class. Her ability to reach her daily goals had definitely improved in three weeks.

Kaylene moved back to the desk, tidying up before she left for lunch, distributing friendly good-byes to the students.

"Hey, Coach!" Ralph's loud greeting forced her eyes to the door. "Come to see Miz Morales?"

Alex had stepped into the classroom. Folding his arms across his chest, he acknowledged Ralph, and two other athletes who were on their way out, but had paused to talk to their coach.

"Six weeks tests are this week. I talk to all the freshman teachers, Ralph. I like to know if I'll be making changes on the team. Do you know if you'll be on the field next week, Ralph?" Alex's voice hinted a playful sarcasm, but his eyes held a warning to the boy.

Kaylene watched the three athletes avoid his commanding stare. They were children being warned by a paternal figure they feared and respected, a special relationship with his athletes she could almost envy.

"Yeah, Coach. I'm doing okay." Ralph nudged the boy beside him. "Come on, Franklin. I'm hungry."

The boys hustled each other along, anxious to get away from Alex's scrutiny. He nodded politely to the last few students who straggled out, then focused his attention on Kaylene.

She squeezed her hands together. She didn't expect the note she left in his faculty mailbox this morning to have such quick results. "Don't you have lunch duty?"

"I got someone to cover for me. I figured this talk was important, or you wouldn't have left a note." In five steps, he was beside her. "I hope this isn't personal business."

The impatient tap of his foot annoyed her. Did he think she made-up this excuse to see him during school hours? She gave him a look like she gave a student who displeased her.

"My note said I needed to discuss some of your athletes. Someone advised me to talk to you about their grades. Don't teachers confer with coaches at school?" No wonder teach-ers didn't like to talk to coaches. They made you feel like you were imposing on their precious time when you were only try-ing to help. "I won't keep you long. I know you're busy."

He slid his hips onto the edge of her desk. "I can always make time to talk about my athletes." His hands rested on his thighs. A smile touched his lips as he studied her. "I like your pink sweater, Miz Morales."

She didn't let his compliment sway her mood, struggling to distance herself from the scent of his cologne, and the appealing movements of his body under his fitted dress shirt and tight brown slacks. She reached for her grade book and held it between them.

"Some of your athletes are failing English."

Alex's approach shifted immediately. "Are we talking defi-nite failures or borderline cases?"

Kaylene pulled a sheet of typing paper from her book. "Last night, I made a list." She handed it to him.

He scanned the paper quickly. "You've got most of my defensive line on this list."

"Alex, a lot depends on the six weeks' test. Those that haven't done homework, may not have enough points even if they pass my exam."

"Six weeks' tests are Friday." He cast aside his relaxed position on the desk and stood up beside her. "Do you want the boys to make up the missing homework or what, Kaylene?"

"They had two weeks to make-up work. I also gave out extra credit assignments, which none of them did." Kaylene released an exasperated sigh. "I spoke to one of them indi-vidually, and he thinks he's going to slide along with his charming personality and talent on the football field."

Alex's disappointed frown transformed him into the gruff Coach Garrison she had first met in the hallway. "Next time, tell the coach immediately if you spot a problem, especially a cocky attitude." His hard look pierced through her. "You should have talked to me sooner. This conference is pointless now."

His impersonal attitude made her blood pressure rise. "I only wanted you to know that some of your players may fail my class, Alex."

"I've been seeing you every weekend for three weeks. We've spoken on the telephone almost every other day. You waited until the end of the grading period to tell me about my players? Why didn't you tell me sooner?"

Kaylene tossed her grade book on the desk. "I'm sorry. The subject never came up!" What was she supposed to do? Ask him to pass the butter, and explain why Franklin can't read? Mention Cesar's test grades while they slow-danced at the University Center? Interrupt a kiss to discuss Ralph's laziness?

She shoved her fists into the pockets of the pink sweater Alex liked so much. "You knew your football players were in my class. Why didn't you ask about their grades when we were alone?"

The paper crunched in Alex's hand. She saw his Adam's Apple pop as he swallowed. "I'm sorry. This is a stupid thing to argue about." He stepped back, and carefully folded the paper, avoiding her by watching his hands. "I'll talk to the boys about studying harder for their English test. Thanks for bringing this to my attention."

The professional courtesy Alex extended was so cold and impersonal, Kaylene shivered. She regretted her plan to keep this discussion on a professional level. They stood in a classroom, a dignified barrier of propriety between them, when all she wanted was some privacy and the opportunity to embrace him.

Kaylene moved to the drawer to get her purse. "You—" She cleared her throat. "Thanks for coming by, Coach. I apologize for any inconvenience—"

"Kaylene, I—" His voice was almost a groan.

She made herself open the drawer, and pull on the black straps of her purse. If she looked at him now, she'd crumble.

"Listen, we can't talk now. I'll come by your place after practice." He used a discreet tone.

Using her purse like a shield, Kaylene turned to face him. "Whatever."

"We'll discuss this tonight, Kaylene." His eyes glided over her. "Please don't worry."

His gentle manner couldn't replace his touch, but she accepted it gratefully, just the same.

"I'll see you later," she whispered. "I can fix us something to eat too."

His fingers raised in a brief salute, then he turned and left the classroom.

Kaylene sighed deeply. She failed to keep the professional separate from the personal. Yesterday, things seemed so black and white. She didn't count on the shades of gray in between.

—∞—

When Kaylene opened her apartment door near eight that evening, she wasn't expecting such a sad, tired scowl on Alex's usually cheerful face. "Am I still welcome?"

"You look like you lost your best friend," she said.

He stepped inside and closed the door. "Let's hope not."

Before Kaylene could move away, he pulled her into his arms and held her tightly. She leaned against him, his green nylon jacket cool on her face.

"I acted like a jerk today, Kaylene. I'm sorry."

"No, I'm sorry for not talking to you sooner. I just didn't think about it. When we're together, I forget you coach my students." She stepped back and cupped his face in her hands.

"I'll be glad and discuss each student with you now, if you want."

His eyes traveled her face. "Discussing my students is the last thing I want right now." He leaned down and kissed her.

Her arms slid around him as she complied wholeheartedly. She welcomed the shelter he provided from her uncertainty, her doubts, and her fears.

"This is wonderful, but if we don't stop, I'll die from hunger." His chuckle tickled her ear.

Her palm thumped his shoulder. "I knew it! You just came here for a free meal!" She pulled back and regarded him playfully. "Grab a kiss, eat, then run. Right?"

"Can I get anything else besides a kiss and some food?" His grin tempted her to share his thoughts, but she didn't commit herself, and pulled him behind her into the kitchen.

"Coaches get a little testy near grading periods," Alex told her after they were seated at the small table. "You caught me off guard today. I just assumed that since you never said anything, everyone was passing. That was stupid of me. I check regularly with the other teachers. I should have made the time to talk to you at school about the athletes."

"I feel awful. You got all the athletes to turn in the book report to Mrs. Dunn. I bet if I had said something, you could have motivated them to do their homework too."

Chewing his food, Alex shook his head. He swallowed quickly. "Homework's different. Lots of kids don't think it counts much. A book report means big points, an important grade. Even I'm guilty of emphasizing the big stuff over the daily work."

Kaylene poured Alex a second glass of iced tea. "What happens when some of the football players fail?"

"You make adjustments. It's not the end of the world, Kaylene." Alex lightly tapped on his glass with his fork. "Sometimes, it helps the second-string players get a chance."

A hopeful flame warmed her heart. "Do your second-string players ever get to make touchdowns?"

"Anyone on a team can make a touchdown. It's like anything else. You just need to be at the right place at the right time." Alex continued eating.

She and Alex had started off in the wrong place at the wrong time, yet managed to move in the same direction. Could they make a touchdown in their relationship too?

Kaylene smiled to herself, wondering when her affections for Alex had deepened into love. Her heart beat with excitement whenever she thought of him. Her mind overflowed with memories of their moments together, and at night, she dreamed of making their relationship a permanent part of her life.

She looked across the small kitchen table and saw the man she loved. She hoped Alex and Kaylene could score big points for love, because in her eyes, they made a great team.

—���—

Alex parked his car in the driveway behind Kaylene's. He turned off the ignition, and sighed tiredly. The effects of the adrenaline pumping through him during the freshman game earlier this morning had worn off, and now the lack of sleep from scouting two out-of-town games was catching up with him.

He had been so proud of his team. Burbank's opposing line easily outweighed each Leon Creek athlete by twenty pounds, but his boys had fought hard, and they had won, 12-7. Now he was trying not to dwell on the fact that his team would probably be different once the failure list appeared on Monday.

Alex got out of his car, and walked up the sidewalk to her apartment. This late lunch with Kaylene was a welcome respite from football games and failing grades. He broke his own promise when he allowed himself to grow attached to her company like this, but it didn't matter. Kaylene had become too important to him.

Immediately when she let him into the apartment, Alex knew something had changed between them.

Kaylene quietly went through the motions of serving them rice, beans, and cheese enchiladas. He slowly ate his salad, wishing she'd explain why her eyes wouldn't meet his. Even their kiss in greeting was a fleeting wisp, as if it pained her to be close to him.

Finally, he put down his fork. He reached across the table and covered her hand. "Is something wrong?"

"Wrong?" she squeaked, then cleared her throat. "No, nothing is wrong, Alex. I'm just tired. I was up late last night."

"So was I. I drove to Brownsville and back last night. I should be at home sleeping, but I came over because I wanted to see you."

"Are you sure you didn't come because I make a mean enchilada?" Her hollow joke fell flat between them.

"Kaylene, look at me." His order made her jump.

Gradually, she responded. "It's about Ralph."

Alex waited, but she offered no other explanation. *Who is Ralph?* His brain flipped through past conversations. *Did I miss something about some guy named Ralph?* He squeezed her hand gently. "Yes? Go on."

"He's two points short."

The guessing game wrenched Alex's patience. "What are you talking about?"

She pulled her hand away. "Ralph Hernandez. His average is 68. All your other players passed English but Ralph." She raised and lowered her shoulders in a huff. "Don't you see the problem?"

The last thing he wanted to think about was his football players. As he had left the game today, he had wondered if his team would ever win again after the failure list hit his desk. He had made himself squelch his dismal outlook in order to be a better companion for Kaylene tonight. Now, she had brought up the matter, and his bitter feelings resurfaced.

"Now I know I lost one player." He let her hand go and picked up his fork. "I'll replace him on Monday." He really didn't want to discuss it any further.

"I really believed I could make a difference," Kaylene said. She slouched into her chair and sighed. "I was dumb enough to believe I could reach each kid. Find a way to motivate the student no one else could."

Kaylene's destructive mood grated on his nerves. Her disappointment was only made worse by a feeling that she had let Alex down. He knew her grading system was fair and she worked hard for her students. Why was she dragging herself down?

"Kaylene, who's to say you didn't motivate Ralph? You didn't have him the entire six weeks. Mrs. Dunn needs to share some of this guilt you're piling on top of yourself."

"I feel so awful that everyone can't pass my class."

His fork clattered onto his plate. "How do you think I feel failing kids in P.E.? P.E.! Anyone should be able to pass P.E.! It's not like I require them to bench press two hundred pounds or be able to run a mile in five minutes. All I ask them to do is dress out and participate, know the rules of the sports we play, and pass an easy true-false." His tone sharpened. "Do you want me to yell at you because Ralph failed your class? Call you a lousy teacher? Would that change anything?"

Tears glistened in her eyes as she blinked at him.

He rubbed his forehead, trying to reclaim his temper. "I'm sorry. This is not a good time to discuss failures. I've had four hours sleep, I'm hungry, and I'm angry because you insist on blaming yourself for something you can't control. I love you! And I won't let you convince yourself you're a bad teacher because one football player was too lazy to do homework!"

Her face opened up, from the raised eyebrows to the expanse of glittering eyes. Her mouth rounded in surprise.

Realizing he blurted out his deepest feelings in the middle of his tirade, he clamped his lips together. But there was no way to take back anything he said when each word was the truth. He did love Kaylene. She had become a treasured part of his life right now. The challenge of coaching made him reach for the highest goals, but his victories were empty without her support and love.

Kaylene's face relaxed into a smile. Shyly, she lowered her eyes and picked up her fork. "I think we should eat, then you can nap on my sofa while I do dishes."

"Good idea." Only he wanted to tell her she could do dishes after he left. If he sat on the sofa, he wanted Kaylene beside him. He wanted to spend as much time as he could with her. Because of Kaylene, he had begun to reconcile the demands of his career with the needs of his heart.

He couldn't predict Kaylene's perception of her life as a coach's girlfriend. Since she didn't respond to his admission with her own expression of love, he guessed she wasn't certain if a football coach was worth loving at all. He could only hope she might like to try.

Chapter Seven

Kaylene dropped the dish towel on the sink. She should have told him. After he admitted his love. After dinner. Before he fell asleep on the sofa. Before he zoomed off to the game. She should have told him, "Alex, I love you too." But, she hadn't.

At first, she was too surprised to respond. Once the words sunk in, they were busy eating, and it didn't seem right saying, "I love you. Want some more beans?"

Then she had sent Alex to the living room, promising to postpone dish washing and join him. She left him only long enough to put away the leftovers, but when she returned, he was asleep on her sofa. She watched him sleep, enjoying the peaceful look on his handsome face. When he awoke, he exclaimed he was an hour late, and rushed out with a quick kiss and the news that he wouldn't see her tomorrow because he'd be working on his own grades.

She looked out the small kitchen window, feeling as lonely as the bare branches waving in the autumn winds. She yearned for Alex's company, his love and warmth. There didn't seem to be enough hours in the day for them to be together. If only the nighttime was theirs to share as well.

If only she had told him, "I love you too, Alex."

The ring of the telephone startled her. Still lost in thought, she walked to the living room.

"Hello, *mi 'jita.*"

Kaylene's mood brightened with the Spanish endearment and her mother's tender voice. "Hi, Mom. I'm glad you called."

"You sound sad. Is something wrong?"

Kaylene could imagine the worry creasing her mother's brow. "I'm only tired. I stayed up last night to average grades." She plopped down on the sofa. "Some of the kids failed my class and I feel bad about it."

"But, Kaylene, this is only one grading period. They have the rest of the year to bring up their average! Don't blame yourself if they don't study and do homework."

Kaylene smiled. "That's what Alex told me."

"Alex? You mention him every time we talk now. Is it serious between you?"

"He's a very special man." Weeks ago she had told her mother about the fight and showering him with mop water. His name had crept into their weekly phone conversations more than she realized.

"Your father and I will be in town next week for your cousin's wedding. Why don't you ask Alex to take you? I told your brother just last week that you and Alex were dating. He said it didn't surprise him that Alex went into coaching. He said Alex had always been good in sports."

"Is Pat coming in for Carmen's wedding?" Kaylene changed the subject. She wasn't ready to discuss her feelings with her mother until she discussed them at length with Alex.

"No, Pat said he couldn't make it." Her mother's voice rose sharply. "I hope you don't feel pressured to rush into marriage, Kaylene."

Since her teenage years when Kaylene first began dating, her mother had preached the dangers of marrying young. She had always stressed the importance of getting an education, establishing a career, and then finding the right man to share her life. As Kaylene's high school friends staged lavish weddings, and most divorced only a few years later, her mother's commentaries expanded into waiting until the right man proposed to be sure the marriage lasts forever.

Kaylene's heart now beat with the hope that the right man had slept on her sofa only an hour ago. If they could get a real chance to talk, maybe she'd have her own chance at forever.

—⟨⟨⟨—

Kaylene rushed through the crowded halls. She'd overslept, and was scared she wouldn't make it to her classroom before the bell rang. Troubling thoughts had kept her awake last night. Of all the students who didn't pass, Ralph was the one who worried her most.

"Miz Morales!"

Kaylene stopped, glancing around. The hallway was thick with moving bodies bumping into her. She choked the briefcase handle as Ralph pushed his way up to her.

"How did I do on the test?"

Kaylene looked up and saw anticipation shining in his black eyes. She hated to disillusion him. "You passed the test, but you failed the six weeks."

"That's stupid! How can that happen?" Hands on his hips, he growled at her. "How can I pass a test and not pass the six week?"

His nasty tone irritated her. She was also impatient to leave. "Ralph, I told you several times that you needed to do your homework, which you didn't. You barely passed the test. When I averaged everything together, you were two points short."

"Two points?" His voice was a roar. "I'm going to fail because I'm two points short?" He glared at the students who paused to watch. The audience only seemed to make him angrier. "Come on, Miz Morales. It's just two lousy points. Give 'em to me."

"I'm sorry, Ralph, I can't do that. You should have done your work."

"This grading system of your stinks!"

She raised her chin and spoke in a cold, distinct voice.

"I won't discuss your grade any further, Ralph."

He uttered a vulgar curse, spun around and stalked away, roughly pushing through the students like a human battering ram.

The warning bell rang loudly. Kaylene knew she couldn't worry about the confrontation now as she hurried up the stairs.

"Sleep late this morning?" Sandy Ramirez grinned as Kaylene unlocked the door.

A boy's comment came from behind her. "She stayed up late to give us all A's."

"You wish!" Kaylene jerked open the door.

Everyone rumbled in as Kaylene dropped her briefcase, two heavy books, and her purse on the teacher's desk. She quickly tried to organize herself for first period. It was more difficult because so many students interrupted her, curious to know their grades. She finally went to the blackboard and wrote: "Don't ask me about your grades. I'll tell you when I'm ready."

For each period that day, she responded as a teacher. But she also acted like a counselor as she talked to several students about their grades, encouraging them to work harder.

Then she went on to announce the next unit of study, Shakespeare's *Romeo and Juliet*. Kaylene didn't let the complaints dampen her enthusiasm. She had a few tricks ready for her freshmen to enjoy Shakespeare.

In fourth period, she treated Ralph like the others who had failed, but her advice was turned back with a fierce scowl. She was grateful he didn't cause a scene or challenge her again.

With a new unit of study, she felt optimistic she might be able to reach those who hadn't passed and give their grades a boost upwards. Even someone like Ralph.

—⁂—

Alex rubbed his jaw as he studied his roster. He needed to readjust positions now that he received official word that Ralph, Paul, Ronnie, and Vincent were ineligible to play football. The four other players he lost usually sat the bench, so their vacancies wouldn't present a problem. He sighed. He would miss Ralph's strength and Vincent's quickness. The smaller guys admired the big lineman. It was a shame the big linemen didn't present a better academic example.

"Can you believe it? I failed! Two lousy points!"

Ralph Hernandez's voice carried over the wooden partition separating the locker room from short hallway to the coaches' office.

Alex might have ignored Ralph's outburst except he heard the words "Miz Morales" followed by a line of obscenity which made the names on his clipboard disappear into a red flash of anger.

"I just don't get it," Ralph continued after his explosion. "If she's sleeping with Coach, why won't she help out one of his best players?"

"Miz Morales and Coach—"

"No way!"

"I saw them, man. I *know* he's getting some—"

"That's enough!" Alex's legs hammered the carpet as he pounced on the group in the locker room.

His loud bark stifled everyone. Ralph clutched his shirt against his bare chest. Ronnie sat on the bench grappling with shoelaces. Chris stopped zipping up his jeans. Franklin, Vincent, and Henry, already dressed, slouched against gray metal lockers. Each froze at Alex's appearance.

Anger tensed every muscle. If those three boys weren't already off the team, he would throw them off right now. "How dare you talk about your teachers that way?" His eyes bored holes into every face gaping at him.

"I heard what you said about Ms. Morales. I don't ever want to hear that talk in here again. Do I make myself clear?" He didn't wait for an answer. His fury pounded like a Texas hurricane hitting the coastline. "I never expected my athletes to talk about my personal life in such a disrespectful way. I might have expected such talk from the other students, but not from my athletes. I thought I could be proud of you on and off the field, but right now I don't want to claim I even know you, much less that I coach you. Speaking of which—"

He popped the clipboard up from his side as he read off a list he had already memorized. "Ralph, Vincent, and Ronnie, clean out your lockers. You're off the team. I'm sure it's no surprise." He pointed at Ralph. "And you! In my office in five minutes!"

Alex's lightning stare enforced the embarrassed silence when he turned and left.

Walking back to the coaches' office, Alex couldn't believe the emotional forces slamming around inside him. Why did he let the boys' talk get to him? None of it was true. None of it mattered. *Come on, Alex. Don't be stupid. It does matter. They were talking about Kaylene. And she matters. A lot.*

"You okay, *amigo?*"

Domingo's quiet voice startled Alex. He didn't think anyone else was in the coaches' office.

Alex threw the clipboard on the desk. "I gave the word to a few players."

"You gave them a few more words than that, Alex."

Alex planted himself in the green swivel chair, then leaned back rubbing his temple. "I just let them get to me, that's all."

Domingo zipped up his nylon jacket. "Kids have a way of doing that. What did they say?" He sat on the edge of the desk.

Alex shook his head. "Just trash. The guys were talking trash about Kaylene, that's all."

Domingo nodded. "I'm glad Sondra isn't a teacher. When I hear the kids mouthing off about one of the women teachers, I sometimes think, what if that was my wife and they said she had a great pair. Could I keep control? I mean, my wife's pears are my business, you know?

Alex eased into a grin. "Yeah, I know."

Domingo slapped Alex's knee. "Don't worry, *amigo*. It's just talk." He rose on long legs and stretched his branch-like arms. "I'm ready to go home and see my wife now. You leaving?"

"Later. I need to see a freshman about his loud mouth." He did appreciate his assistant lightening his load. "See you tomorrow, *amigo*. We'll have a hard day teaching those kids some new tricks."

Domingo shrugged. "That's putting it mildly." He waved as he left.

Alex studied the roster again. When a voice cleared loudly behind him, he swiveled in the chair and found Ralph Hernandez filling his doorway, a denim jacket tightly clenched in his large, brown hands.

"You wanted to see me, Coach?"

"Come in, Ralph, and close the door." After his orders were followed, Alex motioned to a chair.

Ralph flopped down. He stared at the floor.

"I'm very disappointed in you, Ralph. I thought you'd be man enough not to blame others for your mistakes. Ms. Morales gave you the grade you earned. I know she warned you about doing homework."

Ralph's round black eyes shone. "Couldn't you ask Miz Morales to give me the two points? She's your girlfriend. She'd do it for you."

"I don't believe in using my friends like that." He was annoyed Ralph knew about his personal relationship with Kaylene, and he was still furious the boys had discussed their relationship in the locker room. Forcing his personal feelings aside, he kept his mind on academics. "You need to work to get the grades you want, Ralph. I don't know why you blamed Ms. Morales anyway. You didn't pass Coach Cortez's Spanish class either."

"I figured you'd talk to Coach and Miz Morales because I'm the best player you got."

He gave him a long, hard stare. "I can't use anyone on my team with an ego the size of yours, son. If you can't hold up your responsibilities for the team, then you can't play for me."

Ralph moved as if he sat on thorns. "Can I go now?"

"You can go, Ralph."

He bounded for the door, flung it open, and raced out.

Alex knew Ralph's troublesome behavior was the result of others making him an exception. The sooner Ralph realized school responsibilities were important, and someone forced him to accept the consequences of his actions, the better athlete he would be.

Once they both cooled down, he'd approach Ralph about raising his grades so he could play on Alex's junior varsity baseball team next spring. He hadn't given up on Ralph, just given him a taste of discipline, Garrison-style.

Alex rose from the desk, and took his jacket from the rack by the door. He needed to see Kaylene. He had rushed off Saturday, and he couldn't spare time yesterday to see her. He needed to talk to her about their relationship.

Today his heart overpowered his reason. He never cared about anyone as much as he cared about Kaylene and it was time she knew the score.

"I know it's here somewhere!" Dressed comfortably in a worn out sweatshirt and old jeans, Kaylene crawled over the living room carpet to a stack of papers. "Okay! If I start with this, then I—" she paused with a frown, glancing over the piles on the coffeetable. "Now, what did I do with the sheets on personification?"

The doorbell rang.

Kaylene sat back on her heels. She didn't want company. Not when her apartment looked like a file cabinet just exploded. "Who is it?" she yelled, impatiently.

"Alex! We need to talk!"

She jumped up and scrambled to the door, papers bent between her hands. As soon as she opened it, a gust of wind blew Alex through her door and sent the papers on the floor flying in every direction.

With a shriek, Kaylene shoved him aside and slammed the door. She surveyed the ruins of her last two hours of work. "Oh, no. I'll never get organized now!"

Alex's arm slipped around her shoulder. "I'll help you if I can." He squeezed her close to him.

Kaylene added the papers in her hand to the mess, and swung herself around to her put her arms around his waist. She'd worry about Shakespeare later. The unpredictable man she loved had appeared from out of the cold night. She smiled. "We can get to the mess later. I'm glad to see you."

"Even if I interrupted your work? I'm sorry about your papers." His hands stroked through her dark hair. "I wanted to talk to you. Something happened today, and I realized we needed to talk about us."

She tried to read his thoughts by studying his eyes. They focused on her, but she sensed no sadness or anger. She saw them narrow, then close completely as he brought his lips down on hers. His embrace compelled her to forget about everything but him.

He captured her mouth with an intense longing. Every part of her wanted to love him. Sweet pains rocked her, but his powerful arms held her steady. Her silent profession of love would pave the way for the words she needed to say.

"Oh, Kaylene, I love you." His lips brushed against hers as he spoke. "I tried hard not to, but I couldn't stop."

She murmured his name as she touched his chin with her lips. "I love you too. I was scared there wasn't enough time for us to be together. That you didn't have time to love me."

Alex pulled back to look directly at her. "There really isn't time. Not during football season. But somehow it happened." He sighed. "I never want to hurt you, Kaylene."

"It only hurt when I thought you didn't love me the way I love you." She laughed shyly as she admitted, "The way I've *always* loved you, Alex." She reached up to kiss him again, and knew her spirit soared in the heavens when he held her, then kissed her with such passion.

Kaylene slowly pulled away. "Take your jacket off. I'll get us something to drink." Kicking through papers, she made her way to the kitchen. Her heart drummed loudly against her ribs, as shaky hands poured them both a glass of tea. She almost wanted to bathe in the cold drink in the hopes it would slow her pulse.

When she returned to the living room, Alex had picked up enough papers so they could sit on the sofa.

"Tell me about your day," he told her, accepting the tea glass. "How did Ralph take your bad news?"

"He was furious. He thought I should give him the two points." She took a deep breath, then told Alex something he should have known sooner. "Ralph knows we're dating. I think he believed that I would pass him because of you."

He looked more confused than surprised. "How did he even know we're dating?"

"Ralph saw us at the golf course. So did *you* talk to him?"

"Actually, I roared at him." Alex shook his head at his own behavior. "Ralph shot off his mouth in the locker room and I let him have it with both barrels." He placed their glasses on the coffeetable. Then he took her hand, his cold fingertips pressing into her palm. "It made me realize how deeply I love you. In the beginning, I hoped we could be just friends. I tried to distance myself from you."

"Alex, I couldn't figure you out. You'd kiss me or do something special, and I loved it. The next thing I know you'd put up a wall and I couldn't get close to you." She couldn't help laughing out loud. "You make me crazy sometimes."

"Sorry." He offered an apologetic smile. "I kept telling myself not to fall in love with you."

"But, why? It was obvious we were attracted to each other."

"I didn't want to make a mistake. Kaylene, it's tough to get a date during a football season, much less try to build a relationship. The last time I tried, it was a disaster. But I realized you were different. You know, I kept waiting to hear you complain about my schedule, or demand I take you someplace besides a football game. I was so shocked when you put up with my career, and worked on our relationship anyway. I love you so much. I just didn't know how to ask you to share this crazy life I lead as a coach."

"Alex, the only crazy thing would have been if we never tried to love each other at all." She stroked his face. She couldn't think of any reason why they couldn't pass any test of faith in this relationship.

She kissed him, then, to seal her promise of love.

When he smiled, she hugged him tightly, as she celebrated another of Alex's unpredictable moments. He didn't expect to fall in love, and neither did she, but they were a team now. The first half of the football season had its share of setbacks, but now Alex gave her the signal to move forward. Fortified by his love, Kaylene wanted to beat the odds and come out a winner.

—◦◦◦—

"I can see you've gone to a great deal of work." Mrs. Dunn scanned each page quickly. "I never gave figurative language much thought. Do you really expect students to spell *onomatopoeia*?"

"I thought if the students understood why Shakespeare chose the words he did, maybe they wouldn't think it was dumb and boring." Kaylene sat in the first student's desk near the windows while Mrs. Dunn read through her outline for the Shakespeare Unit.

"Do you really expect the students to appreciate Shakespeare's poetic language?" The ice blue gaze fixed on Kaylene skeptically. "I've been teaching freshmen six years, and I've yet to find a group who didn't complain about the way Shakespeare wrote."

"I'm sure they'll still complain. I just thought I'd explain that Shakespeare had to use his words to set a scene because he had nothing else to work with. I don't expect them to suddenly love Shakespeare, but at least I'd give them a reason why he's so hard to read." Clasping her hands together, Kaylene leaned forward. "I thought if the students practiced with the figurative forms before we started Shakespeare, I could squeeze in some composition work before we go into *Romeo and Juliet*."

Mrs. Dunn nodded, still reviewing the outline. Her thin lips were the fine line between approving or censuring her proposal.

Kaylene wondered if Mrs. Dunn would allow a slight digression from the curriculum for the sake of a student teacher who wanted to reach the students in an alternative fashion. Taking a deep breath, she continued. "You told me once that I needed to think like a freshman, not like a college student. I kept that in mind as I came up with my outline. If I break up the reading with short exercises, maybe the freshmen won't get bored. If they practice personification in creative writing, maybe they'll spot it in one of Shakespeare's speeches."

"What's this on the last page about stage dueling?"

Enthusiasm strengthened her self-confidence. "I have a friend in the drama department who's willing to demonstrate how actors prepare for a duel with swords. I think the students would love seeing a real sword fight scene, don't you?"

"Mr. Zachary will never allow those weapons in the classroom."

"Well—maybe I could hold it in the gym or outside on the lawns."

"The coaches teach P.E. in the gym, and the weather's been so unpredictable lately."

"But it would be a great learning experience for the students! Couldn't I ask him?" Kaylene tightly gripped the edge of the desk, trying to keep her exuberance under control. Last week Mrs. Dunn hadn't immediately approved of Kaylene's creative review sheet on connectives, but at the end of the day, told her she thought the unusual sentences helped ease the strain of reviewing for six weeks' tests for everyone. Wouldn't she ever earn Mrs. Dunn's trust?

Mrs. Dunn placed the papers on the desk and folded her hands upon them. She looked at her student teacher. "You can do your Shakespeare unit in the way you outlined, Ms. Morales. Talk to Mr. Zachary, too. I'll support your idea."

"Thank you, Mrs. Dunn!" Kaylene knew she beamed with excitement. "I'll get started on this tomorrow."

"Good." Her supervising teacher picked up the papers and extended them to Kaylene. "I'll be curious to see the results."

"Me too." Stepping forward, Kaylene took her lesson plans. She hoped the students had the curiosity to learn something new about Shakespeare and have some fun too.

The rest of the week moved quickly through writing assignments using various types of figurative language. The students created their own comparisons of unlike objects using similes and metaphors. They insulted each other with hyperboles as they exaggerated faults, qualities, and talents with good natured fun. Only once did Kaylene worry about her two wildcats in sixth period taking the exaggerated teasing too seriously and starting another fight. And this time, she used a calm approach, not a bucket of water, to stop them.

Her classes used personification to describe everything from trees to toilet paper, and made up extraordinary tongue-twisting sentences to emphasize alliteration. The challenge to make statements creatively complicated sparked humor and friendly competition.

Ralph's competitive nature eventually won over his attempts to remain aloof and brooding during class. He never volunteered to read his writing, but allowed Kaylene to share it with the class. His self-esteem slowly returned as others complimented his way with words. A self-satisfied gleam sparkled in his eyes when Kaylene told the class Ralph's personification of a football showed great insight into the game itself.

Kaylene enjoyed the successful teaching activities, and in the evening shared all of her experiences with Alex on the telephone. Each day she honed skills to insure professional success, but the nights invited her to set her sights on personal fulfillment too.

Chapter Eight

Gray, cloudy skies rained down on the wet, muddy freshmen football players attempting to finish a game despite the slippery ball, slushy field, and windshield-wiper weather. The rain pelted the field and the clusters of umbrellas in the stands.

Kaylene shivered under her red umbrella. *Why don't the referees just cancel the game?* There were fumbles because the ball slipped out of players' hands; too many unexpected slides into the muddy grass instead of a quick run across the goal line.

Grimy players stood beside Alex and Domingo discussing strategy. Both coaches wore wet baseball caps and green nylon jackets dripping with water. Their dark slacks were splattered with mud from the sloppy field.

As Kaylene shifted on the hard bleacher, the moisture seeped deeper into her jeans. She glanced around at the wet spectators and wondered why didn't they go home, especially the man with the two small boys sharing a big black umbrella. She sighed, knowing she should go home too, but hated to be disloyal to Alex and his freshmen. She told him she could accept his life as a coach and support his work, but it had been easier to be optimistic and loving when she had been warm and dry indoors.

Suddenly, her bottom vibrated from the thump of heavy feet on the bleachers. She saw three boys clumping their way to the top. She only recognized Ralph. Brushing the rain-soaked black hair from his eyes, he leaned against the iron guard rail, hands jammed into the denim pockets of his blue jean jacket. A scowling glare made him look mean and unapproachable. Was he there to watch the boy who had replaced him? Or had he come in the hopes of watching the team lose?

The game continued with weather related turn-overs, but by third period, Leon Creek managed to score two touchdowns to Kennedy's one.

As the officials ended the game, Kaylene's body shook again from the tight-lipped trio stomping down the bleachers. Dagger-throwing stares attacked the team cheering in a circle around their coaches. She decided all three of the boys must all have been on the team once, but now could only participate as spectators.

Watching them leave, Kaylene saw Ralph pause a moment. His entire body seemed to raise, then lower with his thoughts. She knew he had learned a painful lesson when he realized this team could win without him.

Glancing over his shoulder, Ralph's somber black eyes caught her sympathetic look. He said something to his friends, then came alone to where she stood.

"Came to watch your boyfriend?"

"I came to watch the team. I've been at every game, Ralph. That's how I knew you were such a good player."

"I didn't know that." A wry smile curved his lip. "You must love Coach a lot to sit in the rain for a freshman game."

That idea crossed her mind a hundred times this morning. Thoughts of Alex made her stay, but didn't keep her from feeling cold and wet. She also felt ridiculous for putting herself in a situation that could get her sick.

She still wanted to keep her private feelings out of a conversation with Ralph, so she didn't mention Alex. "I'm here because my students are playing, too. I like to support them anyway I can. Why did you come to the game?"

He blinked at her direction question. "I—" He shrugged. "I don't know. I just came." He started to back away. "See you Monday, Miz Morales." He turned and went back to join his two friends waiting at the bottom of the steps.

"Kaylene!"

She spun around, surprised to hear Alex's call.

He stood on the other end of the wooden stands, motioning to her.

Smiling, she went to where he stood. As she came to him, she wondered why he didn't look happier.

"Congratulations, Alex! The boys did well despite the players you lost."

He nodded, his eyes shiny with pleasure, but she noticed the emotion didn't reach the rest of his face. "Kaylene, I hate to mess up our plans with your parents, but I'm completely soaked. I need to drive home and change clothes. I'll never make it over to your place and be back here in time to leave with the scouting team for Carrizo Springs. I'm sorry."

Disappointment shriveled her insides like the rain wrinkled her fingers. "I'm sorry, too, Alex. My parents are eager to get to know you again. Couldn't we cancel dinner plans? Couldn't you just come by for a short while and talk to them?"

"I'm sorry. Your apartment isn't on my way. I'm pressed for time, Kaylene." He looked towards the gym. "I need to get back to my team now."

She sensed his urgency, and her mood darkened. He always seemed anxious to leave so he could do something for the team. Why couldn't he rush through his work, so he could have time for her? She hated feeling like an imposition on his time.

"Will I see you tomorrow after your Sunday meetings here?"

"I'll try. Give my regrets to your folks, okay?" He stepped back, waved and turned to jog into the gym.

Dropping the umbrella onto her shoulder, Kaylene headed to her car. For the first time that morning, she welcomed the drops splashing over her. She could blame her wet face on the rain, and no one would be the wiser.

—〰—

"Well, at least Alex's team won." Carlos Morales reached for the glass salt shaker and shook it lightly over his chicken and rice. "If my little girl dated a man who didn't win, I might be worried." He winked at Kaylene.

She smiled. Her father's familiar dark face with a grayish-black moustache was a welcome sight across her dinner table.

"I'm disappointed Alex couldn't come by." Helene Morales patted her daughter's hand. "Maybe next visit he can make time for us."

Kaylene didn't miss the message in her mother's words. "It wasn't his fault it was raining so much that he had to go home to change, Mom. Usually, we have two or three hours together before he needs to report to the gym or leave to scout a game. Tonight, he's scouting in Carrizo Springs. It's a four-hour drive."

She sounded like a broken record. Didn't she explain all this when her parents first arrived at her apartment?

"So, I guess you're going to Carmen's wedding alone?" Her mother toyed with the turquoise necklace around her long, graceful neck. She looked so dignified in her simple silver dress. Her hazel eyes had always missed nothing, so Kaylene tried to not to look directly at her.

"It's such a shame Alex couldn't take you."

"It won't be the first time I've gone to a wedding without a date, Mom. Anyway, I won't be alone. I'll be with you and Daddy." Kaylene speared her fork into a piece of chicken. She chewed, but didn't taste it.

"Well, if you continue to date your coach, I expect you'll be going to a lot of things alone." Her father's words were factually stated. "A man who wants a winning team devotes a lot of time to them."

"I guess it can't be any worse than dating a doctor or lawyer," her mother said. "Their schedules keep them away from their families too. At the most inconvenient times!"

Kaylene frowned. "It's not all that bad, Mom. Alex isn't going to get a call in the middle of the night."

"Maybe not, but he's still going to miss family functions because he has to be at a game or something. And what's next? Will we see him coaching the Cowboys someday?"

"I don't think so, Mom." Kaylene saw the amused grin on her father. "He likes coaching high school sports."

"Too bad. He could make a lot of money. And I bet high school coaches don't get time-and-a-half for working extra hours, do they? I never minded when your dad worked overtime, because he was always paid well. What does Alex have to show for his hard work?"

"A winning team, Helene! There's no crime in working hard to reach a goal, even if it doesn't bring you a big salary. If Alex is happy in what he does, more power to him!" Her father reached for the *salsa* and spooned it over his rice. "This is all delicious, Kaylene. Too bad Alex missed a chance to see what a good cook you are!"

Kaylene rubbed her temple. Defending Alex and his job gave her a headache, or maybe sitting in wet clothes for two hours had truly made her ill. Listening to her mother criticize Alex made her head pound. The idea of spending the rest of the night greeting her nosy relatives who clicked their tongue because Kaylene was "so sweet . . . and had no one to marry her . . ." only added to the discomfort.

Kaylene swallowed. Her throat hurt. If she was sick, she promised herself to kiss Alex quite thoroughly and give it to him too. Tonight's misery was all his fault!

———

Dancing slowly with her cousin's boss, Kaylene wondered how she came to be persuaded to dance with this conceited braggart who felt he was doing her a favor by dancing with her. She certainly didn't need a man on her arm to build up her self-esteem.

The scent of her dancing partner's spicy cologne reminded her of the flea spray she used on Tempest. His hands roamed her back like that giant squid attacking the submarine in the horror movie she had seen last night on cable. The guy had talked so much about himself, she could probably write his obituary.

"Hey, Kay? Why don't we ditch the old folks, and go out on our own? We're not far from the Riverwalk. I know this great club with exotic dancers."

Kaylene didn't even want to imagine his idea of *exotic*. "Sorry. My parents are staying with me for the weekend."

Slimy lips slid against her forehead. "Then, I'll call you another time."

She pulled back, wanting to wipe the squid juice off her and spread it over his dark jacket.

In the romantic atmosphere with a spotlight dancing off a glitter ball, he wasn't bad looking, with sandy colored straight hair and dark eyes. Once he opened his mouth, though, she knew why he had been divorced twice.

As she saw his pointed chin lower, she made sure her face was out of range for his thick lips.

"You'd be wasting your time calling me."

"Aw, come on, Kay! Are you married or what?"

Kaylene thought about telling him she was entering a convent tomorrow and this was her last day of freedom, but decided to tell him the truth.

"I'm involved with someone else."

"So where is he?"

"Working."

"If I were him, I wouldn't let you go anywhere without me."

"Well, he's not you, Greg."

"Doug. The name's Doug."

"Sorry, I forgot." She firmly pushed out of his arms. "Excuse me, please."

She was rude to leave him on the dance floor, but she didn't care. She wanted to get away from him before she said something she'd regret. She found her parents talking to some relatives she hadn't seen in five years. She listened to the usual comments about being too skinny and inquiries about her career and marital prospects.

Before Kaylene could stop her, Helene Morales began to tell Aunt Delia and Uncle Ben about Alex.

"My daughter's dating one of the coaches where she teaches. He'd be here tonight, but he's coaching an important game."

Kaylene silently smoothed the front of her green dress, embarrassed by her mother's lie, but let it slip by. It was easier to lie than explain what a football scout does. Since she wouldn't see these relatives for another five years, it really didn't matter what her mother said.

The band started another song, a slow *bolero*, one of her father's favorite Mexican love songs.

"Come on, Helene. Let's dance." As her father led her mother away, Uncle Ben excused himself to get another beer.

Kaylene smiled awkwardly at her aunt, then turned to watch her parents dance.

"So you're a teacher now. I taught for twenty years in Houston. The students said I was very strict." Pride rang in her voice. "Everyone had to work hard for each point he earned. And I worked just as hard as my students. None of this teaching two periods and sitting in the gym like those coaches! You know I don't think I ever knew a coach who could carry on an intelligent conversation about anything but sports. They never talked to us teachers unless they wanted us to curve a test grade so one of their boys wouldn't miss a football game."

"All coaches aren't like that, Aunt Delia." However, Kaylene's loyalty fell on deaf ears.

"And you know, teachers have never been paid what they're worth," Aunt Delia said. "We educate the children who will lead the future, but garbagemen get paid better than we do. We deal with the pressure of raising standardized test scores so the school administrators can keep their jobs."

The woman continued to criticize the evils in the education system, but Kaylene tuned out the static and focused on her parents as they moved gracefully over the dance floor.

She always dreamed of having a marriage like her parents. Affection ran deep in the Morales home, and she remembered her parents embracing, touching, and speaking fondly of each other. When her father was asked to go to Laredo for six months and work in a non-profit government agency, her mom closed up the house, and moved with him, eventually getting a job in the program too. Now they worked together, and shared even more.

In the last month Kaylene realized sharing her life with Alex gave each day a new meaning. She loved his surprises, his tender concern, and his loving support. As her parents danced by, a twinge of loneliness reminded her the man she loved was off scouting instead of holding her. The ache grew in size and intensity until she imagined loneliness was shaped like a football.

Alex groaned as he relaxed into the overstuffed chair in Kaylene's apartment. He never remembered feeling so tired, but being with Kaylene always gave him a lift. "How was your weekend?"

"Shall I tell you about my aunt who thinks coaches are scum or the octopus who made a pass at me at my cousin's wedding?" Arms folded, she stared down at him. "Shall I tell you about my mother who thinks coaches should get paid time-and-a-half for the overtime hours they work?"

"Well, I agree with your mother! After what I've gone through this weekend, I'd like a lot more money than a coach's stipend." He reached up and pulled her down on his lap. "And I don't need the woman I love bitter about things I can't change. Kaylene, you have every right to be disappointed about this weekend, and I have a right to be mad because of things that happened to me, but if we spend the little time we have together in a bad mood, we'll waste a great opportunity to enjoy each other's company." He slipped his arms around her waist. Immediately, he knew the tense form in her arms was not ready to forgive him. "If I've learned anything from the last two days, it's that complaining doesn't change anything."

"Sorry, but I just can't turn my feelings off and on like a water faucet." Her dark brown eyes reminded him of yesterday's storm clouds.

"Like a fool, Alex, I spent the morning watching a football game in the pouring rain. I let my mother tell all my relatives you were coaching an important game instead of scouting far away. I had no one to talk to all afternoon but Tempest. And you blow in here Sunday night and want me to be in a great mood? Well, I just can't do it. Not until I tell you how I really feel!"

Ignoring the high-pitched voice and angry set of her jaw, he said quietly, "And what do you really feel, my love?"

He saw her expression soften until she willingly allowed him to hold her close and ease the strain between them.

Kaylene rested her head against his shoulder and sighed sadly. "Oh, Alex. I missed you so much."

He cradled her closely. "Me too, Kaylene. Me too."

"Tell me about your weekend, Alex. Was it any better than mine?" She sat up and slowly massaged his shoulders.

"We drove to Carrizo Springs in the junior high coach's car. On the way up, a tire blew out, and on the way back, a fan belt busted. I didn't get home until 6 a.m. and reported to the gym at 9:30. David was in a killer mood since Leon Creek lost to Rio Verde, which has a worse football record than we do. I'd hate to be around him next week if we lose to Kerrville. Mmmmm, that feels good, Kaylene."

He closed his eyes as her massage and patient listening eased the tension out of him. If he could come home from a scouting trip or after losing a game to this lovely woman, he'd be so much happier during football season. "I guess your parents left already."

"Yes, at noon."

"I'm sorry I missed them. Really."

"I know you are, Alex. I didn't mean to be so nasty when you arrived." Her lips brushed the base of his throat.

"Tell me about this octopus who made a pass at you. Should I be jealous and go break his eight legs?"

Joy bubbled in her laugh. "It's nice to know you care enough to be a little jealous."

"I'll be glad to show you how much I care." Alex dipped her backwards so he could see her expression. First, he kissed the tip of her nose, then her cheek, and finally, he kissed her soft mouth. Her embraced her and wished the moment would last forever.

—ᘓ—

Monday morning was sunny, yet cool. Another cold front had rushed through Sunday night, pushing away the rainy weather. Alex's appearance, and their precious hours together Sunday night, had the same effect on Kaylene's mood. She was happier than she had been in three days as she smiled at her first period class.

"In Shakespeare's day, *Romeo and Juliet* wasn't a popular play. Can anyone guess why?"

Sandy Ramirez's hand went up.

"Yes, Sandy?"

"I'm sure it was because no one wanted to see two young boys kissing each other." Sandy's brown eyebrows drew together. "I wouldn't. Yuck!"

Everyone laughed, including Kaylene.

Gesturing towards the girl, Kaylene smiled again. "The people in Shakespeare's time agreed with Sandy. Since teenage boys played women, no one liked the romantic stories. Shakespeare's audience preferred the stories of kings in the histories and tragedies."

"I don't see how this Shakespeare junk will teach us anything."

The complaint came from Mark Evans, slouched in his desk in the middle of the room. Since the first day when he left her room and didn't return until the end of the period, he was one student who always tried to push Kaylene's patience as far as he could.

This morning, though, Kaylene was too excited about beginning the play to let Mark bother her.

"You may be surprised by this Shakespeare junk. Tell me something, Mark. Do your parents always approve of the girls you want to date?"

"Are you kidding? They always find some way to tear 'em down! Especially my mom!"

Kaylene grinned, but the students had no idea she was thinking about her own situation with her mother when it came to Alex. "*Romeo and Juliet* is a story about two kids, about your age, who fell in love, but couldn't tell anyone about it." Her look went from Mark's ever-present scowl to the rest of the class. "I would bet that when we finish this story, you're all going to think of a dozen ways their deaths could have been avoided." She returned her gaze to Mark. "You may even learn a few lines of poetry to whisper in your girlfriend's ear some moonlit night."

His frown relaxed into a lopsided grin. When the girls next to him giggled, Mark's freckles darkened against his embarrassed face.

Kaylene clapped her hands. "Okay! Let's get started reading, so we can all find something new to say about love!" She moved back to the desk to get her book and begin reading the play. She prayed her students would keep an open mind about Shakespeare, just as she tried to keep a positive attitude when dealing with freshmen students.

She parceled out roles, choosing the better readers to handle the major characters. She chose to read the nurse's role, and the students seemed to enjoy listening to her interpretation. They didn't know she practiced every night in front of Tempest's cage.

The week continued with only a few snags. When the students grew restless, Kaylene passed out copies of a speech and allowed the students to hunt for figurative language within it. One day, they rewrote the prologue in updated language, and on another, they created new settings for the story and humorous reasons for the families to be feuding.

On Thursday, Kaylene's education professor observed the fifth and sixth period, and complimented her ways of moving through the play without boring the students.

She relived all her nervous moments with Alex late that night. He had called after he returned from scouting.

"I told you the students would make you look good in front of your professor. Down deep, they want to look good too." Alex's supportive tone didn't erase the tiredness in his voice.

"How did things go tonight?"

"I'm just glad Carrizo Springs played in town tonight. It's been a rough week. David is so nervous about Kerrville. When I least expect it, he has a question about something I said in the scouting report. I'll be glad when the game's over, win or lose. By the way, the coaches are gathering at David's house Friday night after the game. Since I'm scouting Kennedy and their stadium isn't too far from your place, I hoped you'd come with me. Would you, please?"

She was too surprised to do more than say, "I'd be glad to."

"These coaches' parties go along with the job. This is the first one I could attend since the season began. The men usually watch the game tape and the wives—well, they sit in the kitchen and talk, I guess. I'm usually in the den. You can tell me later what the women do."

She smiled to herself, happy to meet Alex's colleagues and share another part of Alex's life as a coach.

Chapter Nine

As Alex rang the doorbell of the two-story brick house, Kaylene admired the neighborhood. Even in the dark, she could appreciate the neatly kept lawns and modern houses that marked the new housing subdivision as an ideal place to live and raise a family. Lately, her dreams had taken a domestic swing, and she often thought about places like this to create a home.

The polished oak door opened, and Kaylene smiled at the handsome, black haired man inside.

"Hello, Alex. Glad you made it. Come in! Come in!"

When they stood in the short entrance hall, Alex introduced her to his head coach, David Maldonado.

Seeing the man up close, Kaylene was impressed by his commanding presence. She surmised he was six feet tall, with powerful broad shoulders, and a trim waistline. He'd probably gone from talented high school athlete through college athletic scholarships and finally to coaching students himself. Even though Alex told her he was forty, she would bet he could challenge any of his players and probably win the contest.

"I'm glad to meet you, David." Kaylene's fingers seemed lost in his handshake.

"I understand you student-teach at Leon Creek."

"Yes, that's right."

"Good. Come meet my wife." He turned away and led them towards the kitchen.

Kaylene sensed polite conversation was difficult for him. He had to be so disappointed over tonight's loss to Kerrville. Even Alex had been quiet during their drive over.

A tall, slender woman met them at the entrance to the kitchen. "Alex! I'm glad you came tonight. I haven't seen you since August." She gave Kaylene a sympathetic look. "Freshmen coaches rarely get to our home. David always sends them off to scout games out of the city. I'm Gloria Maldonado." She extended her hand towards Kaylene.

"Gloria, this is Kaylene Morales." Alex told her.

Gloria's hazel eyes twinkled. "I'm so glad to see Alex dating. My husband works his coaches very hard. At least the others go home to a wife. But, Alex goes home to what? Pets?"

Alex's hand rested around Kaylene's waist. "No, no pets. I manage to fit in my own extracurricular activities around football."

"Well, good for you! Come into the kitchen and get something to eat."

The large room was all chrome and white enamel. Beyond the appliances and L-shaped counter spread with various food trays and bowls of chips was an oval table made of glass. Set on white wrought iron legs, six matching chairs surrounded it.

Kaylene smiled as she was introduced to the other coaches and their wives. From the way everyone curiously studied her, she was undeniably the first woman Alex had ever brought to their gatherings. She accepted their speculative glances with good humor, and hoped they'd welcome her into their inner circle.

She noticed when Gloria invited everyone to eat, the men served themselves, then gravitated towards a paneled den to the right of the kitchen. Alex warned her the coaches' gatherings tended to segregate, but she didn't think it would happen so soon. Sipping a margarita, she stood by the glass door pretending to admire the cement patio and square swimming pool, feeling out of place. Everyone else knew one another. She knew only Alex.

Alex's hand at the small of her back gently steered her towards the counter. "Let's eat. I'm starving."

She followed behind Domingo's pregnant wife and started to serve herself cold roast beef, swiss cheese, and a hard roll for a sandwich; tortilla chips and *salsa*, spears of carrots and celery.

"Kaylene, come sit by me," Gloria called. She sat at the table with her drink.

Actually, Kaylene wanted to stay with Alex, but didn't want to offend the hostess. She took her food and went to sit by Gloria although her eyes wistfully followed Alex into the den.

"I don't think Paul has spoken six words since the game ended." A pudgy black-haired woman grumbled as she sat down across from them. Her heavily made-up eyes fluttered on Kaylene. "So, where do you work, honey?" She fluffed her curly hair with her fingers.

Kaylene didn't know whether to eat, as neither woman had any food before her. She toyed with a chip. "I teach at Leon Creek."

"That's convenient! If I worked where my husband did, maybe I'd see him once in a while."

"Eva, even if you worked at the same place, you'd never see Paul." The sarcastic response came from a petite redhead dressed in black. She placed a plate with chips and salsa in the center of the table. "I was secretary at Highlands the same year Steve coached with old man Bennett. I think I saw Steve once at lunch time, but only because he locked his keys in the trunk of his car and needed mine." She took the chair beside Kaylene.

Domingo's wife appeared at the table with her own plate of food. She sat down by the black haired woman. Her pregnant condition was more obvious because she was as tall and thin as her husband. "Domingo and I try to reserve Sunday evenings together."

"Don't you just hate having to make an appointment to see your own husband? No offense, Gloria, but David works his coaches longer than any other Paul has worked for," Eva said.

Gloria shrugged helplessly. "He likes to win."

"It may be time to change strategy! This will make another weekend I'll get the silent treatment from Paul. It's not my fault they lose, but you'd think so, the way he acts." Eva swallowed the rest of her margarita in one gulp.

The redhead reached for a chip, then looked at Kaylene. "How does Alex find time for dating? During football season, coaches hardly see their wives and we live with them." She frowned. "Steve wasn't even there when our third daughter was born, Sondra."

Rubbing her stomach, Sondra laughed. "I timed this baby to arrive after football and just before track season starts."

Eva grunted. "I went into labor one game. Paul asked the trainer to drive me to the hospital. Here I am puffing away, and this kid fresh out of college is telling me about some childbirth film he saw in health class. He was disappointed the nurses wouldn't let him in the birthing room."

"Aren't you hungry?" Gloria patted Kaylene's hand. "Please don't wait on us. We eat like normal people do at regular hours. It's our husbands who eat after the games."

"Except for me. I eat whenever I can!" Sondra exclaimed, as she enjoyed a square of cheddar cheese.

Kaylene smiled at Sondra. She didn't seem to be as bitter as the others. "Is this your first baby?"

"The first of many, I hope." Waving a stalk of celery, she continued talking. "Both Domingo and I want a big family. I get lonely when he's working, so the kids can keep me company." She laughed happily, but no one else joined her.

The idea of substituting children's company for a husband's didn't appeal to Kaylene. She ate her sandwich slowly, listening to the conversation. A picture of a lonely life as a coach's wife was being painted by women who lived it.

"Babies are great, but my daughter's starting to ask why her daddy can't come to her school and meet her teacher." The red-haired woman sighed. "I hate to think what'll happen when Steve Jr. starts playing soccer next year, and his daddy never comes to his games."

"I've been through that, Carol." Gloria rolled her cold glass between her hands. "Both of our boys gave up soccer and started playing baseball since David wasn't so busy in the spring."

"Where are your children?" Kaylene asked Gloria.

"With their grandmother. David and I agreed not to have them underfoot when the coaches come over."

"That's because they wanted to watch a Disney video last time instead of the game tape on the VCR. Actually, I agreed with kids. Why watch a game over and over again? The ending is still the same." Eva stood up. "Anyone else want another margarita?"

Kaylene shook her head. She noticed Alex returning to the kitchen, a look of weariness slanting his features. He discovered her gaze, and gave her a brief smile.

"Alex, I understand your team is on a winning streak," Gloria said cheerfully. "David says you're doing a very good job handling the freshmen."

Alex shrugged off the praise. "I have some smart kids who make me look good."

"Steve told me you had a big kid who was making a real difference on your team, but he flunked English." Carol's long fingernails clicked on the glass table top with a castanet's rhythm. "Couldn't get the teacher to give him a break, huh?"

The food in Kaylene's mouth suddenly tasted like cardboard with a touch of mustard. She reached for her drink to wash it down, so she could defend herself.

Alex's voice came from behind her. "Actually, that same kid flunked Paul's Spanish class too."

"Well, that's a first! I didn't think Paul ever flunked the jocks!" Eva said, with a wry laugh. One black eyebrow raised at Kaylene. "Do you teach any of Alex's team?"

Alex answered for her. "Most of them. She's the English teacher who gives her students grades they earn, even my star players."

A flaming arrow of embarrassment shot through her. Although she was justified in failing Ralph, she didn't want her actions put under the microscope by others who knew nothing of the anguish she suffered. Why did Alex even mention her role in the situation?

"Well, you have more guts than I ever would!" Sondra Reyes remarked, her face revealing her surprise, even admiration.

"If I was a teacher, I'd never teach where my husband coached. Football intrudes on our marriage enough as it is." Eva returned with a new margarita. "Maybe you and Alex can keep your priorities separate, but I never could."

Kaylene said nothing. She noticed Alex leave the immediate area to refill his plate, and returned to the den without a glance in her direction.

Initially, when he had asked her to this party, she was excited. She grabbed the opportunity to spend time together on a Friday night, and get a chance to meet the people with whom he worked. She didn't think Alex would spend the night in a different room, and leave her among the women who had nothing positive to say about life as a coach's wife.

Was this the future she wanted? Gathering with others to complain while your husband watched films of games his team lost? Sending your children away from their beds so they wouldn't bother their father? Timing your pregnancy so your husband could be present for the birth of your child? Her thoughts raced over the negative aspects of marriage to a man whose career was coaching. Her romantic dreams were getting ripped apart by everyone around her.

The coaches finished dissecting the game near 2 a.m. Kaylene had spent three hours listening to everyone's stories about living with a coach.

By the time she sat in Alex's car, she had serious doubts about her relationship with him. She didn't want to accept second place in Alex's life for three or four months of every year. She wanted her husband to share her life, not grab a quick piece of marriage in between games.

As she stared out the window of Alex's car at the pretty neighborhood, she sighed. *If Alex and I did buy a nice house like these, would he ever have the time to enjoy it?*

"I'm sorry it's so late," Alex said, driving easily with one hand. "I should have left earlier, but David was in one of his moods. He was awfully depressed tonight."

"Maybe they'll win next week," Kaylene offered, although she really didn't care. She was sick of football talk.

"I doubt if they'll win next week. Carrizo Springs is tough. They'll have a better chance against Kennedy. From what I scouted tonight, it should be an evenly matched game." His voice changed. "So, did you have a nice time?"

"Fine." She continued looking out the window. "The ladies are nice people. I can't say much about their husbands. I didn't talk to any of the coaches tonight. Including you." Her chilly voice was a message in itself.

They drove back to Kaylene's apartment in a tense silence.

Even though she and Alex were together, a spirit of loneliness haunted her. This had happened before, but usually when his attention as a coach forced her out of his thoughts.

This time, her preoccupation separated them, making her feel like she was the only one riding in the dark.

She turned to Alex, his handsome face serious and thoughtful. Her heart split apart when she considered how much she loved him, yet couldn't accept the limitations his job placed on their relationship.

When he parked his car in her driveway, his sigh seemed to fill the gap between them. "When football season is over, I'm going to sleep a whole weekend away."

Kaylene unbuckled her seat belt. "After tonight, I wonder if all the work is worth it. You drive all over Texas scouting teams and Leon Creek still loses. What's the point?"

"You learn from mistakes, and you try again next year."

She stared at the frowning Alex, whose hands were still on the steering wheel.

"I don't think it means that much to me, Alex. I don't think it ever will."

Slowly, he turned to her. His arm moved along the back of the seat. "Do you mean football?" With only the dim illumination from her porch light, she saw the gray embers smoldering in his eyes. "What are you trying to say, Kaylene?"

"I don't care about a sport that means so much to you."

"Kaylene, no one says you have to like football. I bet none of the coaches' wives enjoy football."

"Alex, I don't know if I want the kind of life those women described for me tonight. For several months a year, you'll have to fit me in between a football schedule. I don't like the idea of second place. And I'd like to have an escort to family functions. I'd like to have the man I love available to visit with my family. I want someone who comes home before I'm in my pajamas."

His fingers stroked her hair, then wrapped themselves among the layers. "I love you, Kaylene. I love you more than I've ever loved any woman."

Tears stung her eyes. "I love you too, Alex. But I need you to be part of my life. I need to know that the game of football doesn't squeeze me out of your thoughts. I need you with me, not in some football stadium."

"Kaylene." He swallowed hard as his eyes burned into her. "I love you. I enjoy my job. I can't chose between you."

A whirlwind of emotions spun her into his arms. Clutching his jacket, the tears spilled down her face as her body shook with the anguish of her thoughts. He covered her with his embrace, but it couldn't shield her from the raw pain ripping her in two. She loved him, but how could she separate the man she loved from the coach, who set high standards for his team, when it was the two roles which gave him so much happiness?

There weren't enough words to adequately describe her feelings, so she said nothing. She accepted his gift of comfort and loved him for knowing what she needed most desperately at this moment.

His words echoed between her sobs. "I should have listened to my own warning."

She nodded, feeling his damp jacket slick against her face. Through her shaky emotions, she pulled back to study him.

His large hand wiped her cheek with a delicacy she didn't know he possessed. "I love you, Kaylene. If you want to talk about this further, you'll know where to find me."

His statement only emphasized the hurdles between them. There was no doubt she could find him in a gym or at a football stadium. The problem remained that there was no place for her when he was there.

—⁓—

"You okay, *amigo*?"

Domingo's voice pulled Alex from the dark caverns of his painful thoughts. He blinked into the concerned frown of his football assistant.

"I'm fine. Why?"

Domingo's fingers combed through his straight black hair. "If my memory serves me correctly, we just beat Uvalde. Yet, you're sitting here in the office with the same expression David wore last night at the party."

Turning in his swivel chair, Alex started to rearrange the pencils on his desk. He had a new perspective on his head coach's feelings. Last night, Alex, too, felt the frustrations of a game he couldn't win. Just like David sent out scouts, practiced the boys, and called the plays he thought would guarantee a win, Alex gave Kaylene his support in her teaching endeavors, treated her with love and kindness, and gave her every free moment of attention he could spare.

Sometimes, all you had to show for all your efforts was the emptiness of failure.

"Ask me to mind my own business, but did you and Kaylene have a fight or something?" Domingo sat on the edge of the desk. "I don't think I saw her at the game today."

Alex looked up, grasping at anything he might have missed. "Did your wife say anything about last night's get-together?"

"Like what?"

"I don't know. What the wives talked about, I guess."

"Sondra told me everyone was depressed because Leon Creek lost. She said no one did much but complain about life as a coach's wife. When a team loses, no one has anything good to say." Domingo shrugged. "It's just talk. No one takes it seriously. Next week, we'll win, and everyone will be celebrating, kissing, and hugging like one big family. It's what we are, you know. You get pretty close to people in this job."

The insight helped Alex understand Kaylene's emotional outburst, but he still blamed himself for neglecting her. He wondered if she was rejecting him totally when she had said she couldn't accept his job.

Kaylene had told him football squeezed her out of his thoughts, but today, as her tears haunted him, he could barely think about his football game. He did the job he was paid to do, but for the first time in his career, he started to wonder if the reward was worth the sacrifice.

—⁓—

Perched on the edge of the brown leather office chair, Kaylene hoped she had convinced the vice-principal of her plan. "The college drama students will spend the day at the school and demonstrate stage dueling during the periods I teach."

Ernest Zachary watched her through his glasses. His blue eyes never left her face as he listened. "My biggest concern is the safety of the students. I'd like them watching the demonstration from a distance." One pudgy forefinger tapped his round chin. "If you take the kids to the gym, they'd be able to watch from the bleachers. This would also give more room to the dueling swordsmen."

Kaylene nodded, although he basically repeated everything she had suggested only five minutes earlier.

"I'm sure Coach Reyes and Coach Garrison would welcome the opportunity to show their P.E. students something besides the usual indoor sports. I assume you'd have no objections to their classes watching the demonstration with yours."

"Of course not." She responded quickly, but just like swallowing bitter medicine, a fast gulp rarely prevented an aftertaste. She tried not to think about spending one whole day in Alex's gym.

Kaylene stood up to leave. "Thank you, Mr. Zachary."

"You're welcome, Ms. Morales." He nodded, then smiled. "By the way, I received a call Monday from Todd Weaver at Jefferson High School. He said you've applied for a position during the second semester."

Clasping her nervous hands behind her blue sweater dress, Kaylene nodded. "In the English department, sir. The woman's husband is being transferred at Christmas."

"Todd asked for a recommendation, and I spoke at length with Mrs. Dunn. She says you're doing a fine job with the freshmen."

She smiled, relieved to know Mrs. Dunn's professional opinion.

"I told Todd everything she said. I hope you get the job."

"Thank you, Mr. Zachary. Good-bye."

"Good-bye, Ms. Morales."

Leaving the vice-principal's office, Kaylene kept telling herself that staging her educational program in Alex's gym served the best interest of her students. *Remember that.*

Kaylene's stomach tightened into knots. No one had ever warned her a teacher had to submerge her personal feelings and maintain a even-tempered facade for the students who depended on her. She had been naive to think teaching was merely knowledge and creativity. The responsibilities were enormous.

Since the emotional scene in Alex's car two days ago, she had clung to her teaching duties like a drowning victim clings to a white life-preserving ring. She hoped a rescue boat was sailing somewhere on the horizon.

Chapter Ten

"What's this?" Ralph Hernandez looked at the paper Kaylene extended to him as he passed her desk.

The fourth period was over, and everyone was happy to leave for lunch.

"It's tomorrow's scene, Ralph. I want you to read Tybalt's part," Kaylene replied, as if reading Shakespeare was his everyday habit. "You can't take the books home, so I made a copy. You can practice tonight."

"Aw, Miz Morales. I can't read this stuff." His nose wrinkled with displeasure. "Give it to somebody else."

"Ralph, this is one of the most important scenes in the play. I want someone to take this home and practice, so tomorrow's reading will be exciting. I know you can do a good job."

His black stare narrowed. "Why me?"

"I think you and Tybalt have a lot in common, don't you?"

"He's a troublemaker."

"He's also popular with his friends. He takes things seriously, and he's very strong."

"He's the bad guy, isn't he?"

"Ralph, just because you make a mistake in judgment doesn't mean you have to wear a black hat. A bad choice doesn't make you a bad person." Kaylene watched his thoughts rearrange expressions on his face. "Just remember that Tybalt made one stupid choice, and it got him killed. As the readers of this play, you and I are able to talk about his mistakes and use the lessons in our own lives."

She waved the paper in front of him. "Please, will you do this for me, Ralph?"

He snatched the paper from her fingers. "All I got to say is you better not pick a wimp to be Romeo in this scene. I want it to be a fair fight." For all his bluster, Ralph's black eyes twinkled with amusement, his tough mask cracking before her.

"Thank you, Ralph. In case I haven't told you, I'm pleased with your work this second six weeks."

"You told me, but I like to hear it again." Shoving the paper inside his notebook, he moved away. "Bye, Miz Morales."

"Bye, Ralph." She turned to watch him leave. "Uh—Coach!" The catch of her breath knocked out her insides.

Alex Garrison stood inside her classroom, his gaze focused on both of them.

Kaylene didn't know what to think of Alex's appearance. Since he hadn't called in a week, she wondered if he had given up on their relationship, or had something better to do with his time.

She noticed Ralph seemed just as nervous about Alex's presence as he slowed his pace out the door. "Uh—hi—hello, Coach."

"Hi, Ralph. How are you doing in English lately?" His solemn gaze moved over the boy's shoulder to his teacher.

Uneasily, Ralph glanced back. "Miz—uh—Miss Morales will tell you. I'm getting my grades up."

"Good." He put his hand on the boy's arm. "I heard you've been playing baseball for a church team since you were six. Are you any good?"

Kaylene could almost hear Ralph swallow.

"My coach thought so. Uh—um—We were a good team because we all played together so long."

"I coach junior varsity baseball in the spring. Keep your grades up, and you can try out for my team." He lightly popped the boy's arm. "I'd like to see how good you are."

Ralph looked back at Kaylene, then studied Alex's face. He looked almost suspicious of the two teachers. He must have decided Alex's friendliness was genuine, because he nodded. "Thanks, Coach. I'll be there for try outs." Clearing his throat, he strode from the room.

A natural admiration for Alex made Kaylene smile. "You're nice to give him another chance."

"I'm being selfish. I'd like to win in baseball, and the boys tell me he can really hit." Alex shortened the distance between them. "Besides, in the spring, I won't have to worry about defending your honor when he complains about his English teacher."

Her cordial feelings quickly faded. Alex made her sound like a nuisance in his relationship with his athletes. She realized he wanted her in another school as much as she did, except for different reasons.

Avoiding his look, she shuffled papers on her desk. "Is there something we need to discuss, Coach?" She tried to stifle her emotions by using his professional nickname.

"You left a note for Domingo and me requesting use of the gym on Tuesday. You can have your assembly. It'll be nice to see weapons in the hands of experts for a change."

His attempt at humor didn't lessen the strain between them.

"I'll just have my classes meet me there. I can take roll, and then my friends can do their job. They're going to talk a little about Elizabethan theater, modern theater, and then stage dueling." She spoke in the same professional tone she had used with Mr. Zachary two days ago. She hoped she hid the fact her insides quaked just to have Alex in the same room with her.

"I missed you at Saturday's game." He sounded no different than if he had mentioned a change in the weather.

"I didn't think it was wise to go. Bobby told me you won. Congratulations." She ran out of papers to shuffle. Sighing, she stepped back, and finally looked at him.

His green sweater vest made his eyes appear darker than usual. Almost hypnotically, they pulled her deep inside him. She uncovered the exhaustion, sadness, and loneliness he felt.

For a moment, she was ready to relinquish her personal goals. Love him regardless of the sacrifice. But, he stepped back abruptly, snapping the visual link between them.

"I need to get to lunch duty. David swore ten minutes was his limit. Bye." Spinning on his heels, he walked away from her.

Kaylene didn't bother to watch him leave. She sat down at the teacher's desk and stared out the window trying to recapture her professional calm in the midst of a personal storm.

— ∞ —

Alex rested against the lockers. Taking three deep breaths, he wondered why he put himself through such torture. He never should have volunteered to talk to Kaylene. When he overheard her conversation with Ralph, it only reinforced his reasons why he loved her. She encouraged others to try something different. To look inside, and bring to the surface talents, sensibilities, and emotions no one ever tapped before.

Did she know how much pain it caused him to act so indifferent, when he longed to embrace her and chase away her fears? *Really, Kaylene, there are worse things in life than loving a coach.*

A giggle from a group of girls by the water fountain, reminded him he didn't have the luxury of privacy. Pushing himself from the lockers, his frustration over Kaylene came out in a roar. "Get moving, ladies! You know the rules! You should be in the designated areas during the lunch period." His loud voice echoed in the empty halls, reminding all who heard that Coach Garrison didn't shirk his responsibilities.

Taking the hall at a rapid pace, he walked to the cafeteria.

—⁂—

After a bitterly lonely weekend, Kaylene was grateful to return to school and keep busy with her final week of student teaching.

Tuesday's demonstration in the gym left her feeling pressed for time to complete the play, but she knew the students would enjoy the spectacle of a sword fight. She had received permission from her professor and Mrs. Dunn to return two days next week to complete her work.

Word of Kaylene's demonstration drew a wider audience than she anticipated. Not only were five P.E. classes watching with her English groups, but other teachers stopped in during their conference periods to enjoy the program.

There were two pairs of college students, three men and a woman. Each took a turn lecturing about Shakespeare's theater and explaining techniques used by actors on stage in order to create a realistic fight. Someone narrated while two actors dueled "to the death," and finally, they coached six student volunteers through a mock duel using narrow sticks.

Kaylene was too busy watching students and actors to pay attention to her surroundings or the handsome coach standing by the locker room doors, but at sixth period, Alex's P.E. class volunteered him to be a part of the pretend duel. Unless she wanted to spend the next ten minutes staring at her feet, she knew she couldn't avoid watching him closely. Alex accepted the challenge in the spirit of friendly competition, and Kaylene's friend, Christine, agreed to duel with him.

Before she left the lower bleacher where she had been sitting with Kaylene, Christine said, "He's good looking. I think I'll let him win. Maybe he'll ask me out."

Jealousy chewed up Kaylene's calmness. Her friend was a petite blonde with a bubbly personality. She was graceful and athletically skilled. Her red leotard worn under a pair of gray sweat pants molded her generous curves like a second skin. She'd be a perfect match for Alex any time.

Kaylene carefully watched Christine talking to Alex. Something she said made them both laugh, and after some discussion, Alex and Christine began.

Christine took her position and Alex followed. The wooden swords clicked together as she easily controlled the duel. Eventually, the rhythm increased, and she became more aggressive. Alex's face was tight with concentration.

Kaylene didn't know if she was more shocked that Alex knew the basics of fencing, or more embarrassed because the students wolf whistled and cheered as if they were at a pep rally.

She watched Alex sidestep a sharp thrust, and jump back when Christine charged him again. Her sword cut the air, then clicked loudly against Alex's. He met each blow, then whipped out a counter-move which made the kids cheer. He began to move in, and soon maneuvered Christine backwards as she became the defender, not the aggressor. Then, with a bold swing he aimed his weapon upwards. With a firm crack, Christine's sword flew across the gym.

The students applauded the victory. With a grand bow from the waist, Christine conceded defeat.

Alex retrieved her stick, and walked to where she stood, extending both to her. He offered her a humble shrug, and smiled as if he pantomimed beginner's luck.

"My champion!" Christine announced in a loud, dramatic voice, and with cat-like agility, she bounced forward and kissed Alex squarely on the lips.

The suggestive howls from the students reverberated through Kaylene. She watched Alex's expression blink between shock and anger. His hands clasped Christine's arms, forcing a distance between them. Then he released Christine like she was contagious and walked away.

The school buzzer crackled through the noisy gym, and the students enthusiastically applauded. Kaylene didn't know if they clapped for the unexpected romantic display or the end of school. She saw Alex heading for the locker room. With a purposeful stride, he ignored the students' loud, lewd comments regarding the kiss.

Kaylene made no remark about Christine's behavior although the Elizabethan term *wench* echoed in her mind as she walked the actors out of the gym.

After thanking her friends for the successful program, Kaylene made her way back to the main building. Although everyone's comments about the stage dueling had been positive, Kaylene somehow felt cheated. She knew it had nothing to do with the silly kiss. It was a feeling born from her unsettling personal life.

Without Alex to share her success, her failures, or her adventures with the students, her activities lost a very special quality. The last two weeks had been busy, yet were empty of genuine feeling. She just kept busy to stop thinking about Alex, yet she never really succeeded in blocking him out.

Just walking through the halls reminded her of the day she gave him a bath with mop water. The athletes wrote about Alex in creative writing, and she couldn't go near the cafeteria any more because his forceful presence as a monitor made her hunger for his embrace.

Unexpectedly, she bumped into Mrs. Dunn in the doorway of her classroom. The papers Mrs. Dunn had been holding scattered around them. Both women bent down to retrieve them.

"I'm sorry, Mrs. Dunn. Let me help you."

"Obviously you were daydreaming about something else."

Kaylene stood upright and handed her some papers. "I think I'm just clumsy." The woman's intimidating presence always made conversation awkward.

"Aren't things going well between you and your coach?"

So shocked by the personal question, Kaylene felt herself go numb.

"It's my impression you and Coach Garrison are romantically involved."

Kaylene merely stared. Discussing her personal life with Mrs. Dunn left her with tongue-tied shyness.

"Ms. Morales, didn't they tell you in education classes about school gossip?" Mrs. Dunn asked impatiently, as if she was trying to get Kaylene to say something.

She gave the woman a hard look. "The last six weeks I've realized education classes didn't teach me half of what I needed to know! Excuse me, please." Kaylene moved past Mrs. Dunn and went to the teacher's desk. She regretted the unprofessional tone she had just used, but her emotions were raw and burning. She wanted to get her purse and briefcase and escape any further discussion of her personal life.

"Something's wrong, isn't it?" The heavy steps behind Kaylene indicated Mrs. Dunn was a very persistent woman.

Kaylene took her purse from the desk drawer. "The demonstration today was a big success. And I received a call from Jefferson to meet with the principal next Monday for an interview. Mr. Zachary said you gave me a good recommendation. Thank you, Mrs. Dunn."

"I think you're a very creative teacher."

"Thank you." Kaylene smiled at the compliment, but still couldn't discuss Alex with the woman. She placed the purse strap over her shoulder. "I'll see you tomorrow."

Mrs. Dunn gently caught her elbow as Kaylene passed. "Can I help?"

The question stunned Kaylene. Mrs. Dunn had never shown any friendly concern before today. Now she understood how Ralph felt when Kaylene had tried to be his friend. She was amazed, suspicious, scared, and relieved, all at the same time.

"I don't think anyone can help me, Mrs. Dunn. I'm in love with a man whose job is his priority. I don't like a football shoving me into second place."

"Don't be so melodramatic!" Mrs. Dunn slapped her papers down, and gave Kaylene a disapproving stare. "I was married to a football coach. I was never second place!" She sighed, and suddenly her blue eyes didn't seem quite as cold. "Your love will be the one constant force in his life. He can win or lose a game, but you and he will always have a life together. For four months out of the year, you just share him more. Football never replaces a wife. There's not even a comparison."

Kaylene understood Mrs. Dunn, but still had other doubts. "I don't know if I can share him. How do you handle the lonely nights when he's scouting or playing an out-of-town game?"

"First of all, it isn't healthy to allow your world to revolve around a man. I used those nights to socialize with my own friends. I even developed a new hobby." Mrs. Dunn folded her arms across her ashes-of-roses sweater. "You still have a thesis to write, don't you?"

She continued as if Kaylene hadn't nodded. "And didn't you stop and think about the fact you have a two month summer vacation together and still get a paycheck? My children were the only ones in the neighborhood who had a father home in the summer."

Kaylene mentioned some of her other fears about a long-lasting relationship with Alex. "Didn't your husband miss some of the children's activities because of football?"

"Kaylene, no parent can come to every baseball game or piano recital. Did your father attend every thing you did?"

The pressure in her head began to clear for the first time in two weeks. "No. Sometimes he just couldn't—"

"And you don't love him any less, do you? Kids are marvelously flexible. Of course, much depends on the man. My husband, Robert, never let a loss ruin our time together. We talked about the disappointment, and I listened to ways he might change a player or two, but I always knew football wasn't life and death to him. Now, all men who coach aren't like that. You're going to have to decide if Coach Garrison has enough self-confidence not to take his coaching losses personally."

Kaylene then recalled Alex's way of handling frustrations. He always managed to focus on the positive, and talked about learning from mistakes, and trying again. In her heart, she knew those admirable qualities made him a good coach and a man worth loving.

Mrs. Dunn changed her tone of voice. "Kaylene, your relationship isn't just affected by winning or losing. There are other difficult moments too. Sometimes, you get sick of the booster club dinners, sports banquets, and an extra load of football jerseys sudsing in your machine. You have to listen to the fans curse your husband's coaching because they think they could do a better job. Then there are the years you wonder if he'll still have a job when a new head coach gets hired."

Kaylene listened carefully. Mrs. Dunn had given her different insights into life as a coach's wife. But there were other things which had affected her relationship with Alex the last six weeks, and she wanted to know Mrs. Dunn's opinion. "Did you ever teach at the school where your husband coached?"

"I did the last seven years. We made a great team. I wanted the athletes to qualify for academic scholarships as much as he pushed the athletic ones. The kids learned if they complained about me or my husband, they got an extra assignment or ten extra laps around the field." There was a dreamy quality to her blue gaze. "I like to believe my students learned about a true team effort by our example."

"Your husband sounds like a special man."

"He was. He's been dead four years now, and I miss him very much." She sighed. "Love is so precious. If there's a man somewhere who loves you, take the risk to share his life."

Kaylene nodded as Mrs. Dunn, the romantic, returned to Mrs. Dunn, the experienced teacher. "There isn't a job in the world which doesn't have its share of time consuming responsibilities, Ms. Morales."

Behind all her matter-of-fact answers, it was obvious Mrs. Dunn knew the positive side to loving a man who loved to coach. This conversation had helped Kaylene sort through her concerns so she could make some important decisions.

"Thank you for taking time to talk to me, Mrs. Dunn."

The older woman merely shrugged. "It's my job to guide student teachers. If you'll excuse me, now, I have an appointment at four."

Kaylene nodded. "Thanks again, Mrs. Dunn. I'll see you tomorrow." She turned and quietly left the room.

Kaylene carefully replayed the conversation in her mind. She weighed each of Mrs. Dunn's statements carefully. Had she missed her opportunity to keep Alex's love because she had not been able to get past her own selfish needs?

Her sigh echoed in the empty school hallways.

Chapter Eleven

Kaylene glanced at the clock ticking away the last minute of sixth period on Friday afternoon. Folding her arms across her, she sighed. She knew she could find answers for her personal problems that would be a better solution than Romeo and Juliet's.

"Hey, Miss Morales?"

She reacted automatically. "Yes?"

"Did you get mad when Coach Garrison kissed that girl the other day?" Shannon Wolf asked.

Kaylene just stared at the girl. For the second time that week, she had someone unexpectedly inquiring about her personal life.

The red spikes in Shannon's hair were just as sharp as her question. "Everyone says he's your boyfriend. If some girl kissed my boyfriend in front of the whole school, I'd bust her face in."

"I would too!" Lisa Mendez added, tossing her long black hair over her shoulders.

It was the first time the two girls had agreed on anything in six weeks.

Kaylene hid her discomfort behind a laugh. "I'm sorry, ladies! I don't believe in fighting." She even grinned at the image of Kaylene and Christine fighting in the way Shannon and Lisa had done six weeks ago.

"So go throw mop water on her!" Lisa waved her hand as if she suggested a great alternative.

Kaylene laughed out loud at the action which had marked her first day at Leon Creek, and felt herself slowly starting to relax.

"So are you going to marry Coach Garrison or what?" Shannon's impatient query cut through Kaylene again. Her mouth went dry. How could she respond to a question which had no simple answer? She wiped her damp palms against the front of her wool skirt.

"Just tell us, Miss Morales. Yes or no?"

Taking a quick step back, she couldn't get away from the looks of twenty-seven teenagers waiting for her answer. There seemed to be no sound in the room but Kaylene's pounding heart.

Suddenly, the bell rang. Kaylene closed her eyes, silently thanking the heavens for its timely sound. Still trying to piece together her feelings since she had spoken with Mrs. Dunn, Kaylene didn't want to explain herself to a group of students who weren't ready to handle the flip side of love songs and fairy tales.

Luckily, everyone was eager to leave school on a Friday afternoon. Kaylene escaped back to her desk before she was caught in a stampede. However Shannon stopped to say, "Send me an invitation to the wedding, okay?"

Kaylene's reply was a silent blush, and Shannon cackled with laughter as she strutted from the room.

Mrs. Dunn arrived as the last student left the room, and by then, Kaylene could speak calmly again.

"Did you finish the play?"

"Just barely," Kaylene sighed. "I guess, I'll call the principal at Jefferson and reschedule my interview. I need to review the play Monday and give the test on Tuesday. I'm sorry my unit didn't fit into your schedule better."

"Flexibility is crucial to teaching, Ms. Morales." Although the professional tone was unmistakably that of a supervising teacher, Mrs. Dunn's face looked less threatening. "The library has a shortened version of the play on videotape. I've reserved it for the classes to watch on Monday so you can go to your interview. You can review Tuesday and test on Wednesday."

Relief and gratitude made Kaylene smile. "Thank you, Mrs. Dunn. You've helped me more than you know." There was a double message in her words.

"Good. That's what I'm supposed to do." Mrs. Dunn moved to the windows and frowned at the cloudy skies. "Do you think it will rain tonight? I hate watching a football game in the rain, don't you?"

"Are you going to the game tonight?" Kaylene glanced at the older woman in surprise. Even though she knew Mrs. Dunn's background better, images of the serious woman cheering at a football game were hard to believe.

"I've been to all the in-town games." Her head tilted upwards as she contemplated the grayish brown clouds. "Haven't you?"

"Um—no. I just went to the freshmen games on Saturday. I didn't have a reason to go to the Varsity games."

"You need to be sensitive to school spirit, Kaylene. The students appreciate a teacher who's loyal. The Varsity team needs all the spirited fans they can find. You should go tonight."

After Mrs. Dunn left, Kaylene took her place at the window. Leaning her forehead against the cold glass, she watched the spots of leaves waving in the autumn winds. She wondered about her future beyond this classroom.

Since her eye-opening conversation with Mrs. Dunn, she had wanted to call Alex, but each time, replaced the receiver without dialing. Her heart advised her to discuss her feelings with Alex in person, and she felt her best opportunity would come after Saturday's game. She hoped her selfish fears didn't tarnish his love, or make him doubt her ability to honor a commitment between them. She loved him, she wanted him to be a part of her life.

Kaylene turned back and looked around the classroom. She had learned the last six weeks how she could be resourceful in any situation, even the unexpected challenges. She'd do the same in her relationship with Alex and score a point for love.

—⁂—

Kaylene walked up the center cement ramp of Edgewood Stadium Friday night. She wasn't sure why she had come to the game. Was it because this team had a connection to Alex? Because Mrs. Dunn said she should show more school spirit? Something tugged at her, and Kaylene hoped she could discover an answer tonight at the game.

The Leon Creek Wildcats game against Kennedy Rockets filled both sides of the Edgewood stadium. Cheerleaders led the pep squad in chants about victory as both bands battled to be heard across the field. Student council members from each school stretched large spirit banners across the goal posts. A painted cartoon of a brown wildcat chomping a fiery green rocket in half decorated Leon Creek's break-through, while Kennedy's artists depicted a gold rocket with orange and red flames chasing a yellow cat with a bandaged head.

Kaylene climbed up the stadium steps as Kennedy burst through the paper break-through. Digging her hands into her jacket pockets, she glanced over the crowded stands wondering where to sit.

Then Kaylene saw a tall, pregnant woman waving a red scarf. She did a double-take before she recognized Sondra Reyes smiling at her and motioning to join her.

Carefully maneuvering between knees, small children, and hot coffee cups, Kaylene managed to find a space to sit beside her.

"Hi, Kaylene! I just love that name. I told Domingo if we had a girl, I wanted her middle name to be Kaylene. We just can't agree on the first name." Sondra smiled. "It's good to see you again. Domingo said you always go to the freshmen games, but I work Saturdays."

The friendly chatter made Kaylene feel welcome. She turned to greet the other women she'd met at the gathering two weeks ago, although she remembered only Gloria's name.

Suddenly, from out of nowhere, a small boy popped up in front of Kaylene. He leaned around Sondra's stomach.

"Hey Mom? Can I get a pickle?"

His mother, the coach's wife with the black curly hair, was on the other side of Sondra. "If you get a pickle, you'd better finish it. Last time you stuck the leftovers in my purse and I didn't find it for three days!"

Laughter from everyone made the boy smile.

"I'll eat it all. Thanks, Mom!"

Before she knew it, the boy had disappeared.

As everyone rose for the playing of the national anthem and school songs, Kaylene noticed the two boys next to Gloria munching popcorn, and the thin red-haired girl talking to an overweight teenage girl. She looked like a sister to the boy who asked for a pickle.

"I'm glad you joined us tonight."

Kaylene turned around to see Gloria Maldonado smiling.

"David says if the team wins, he's treating the families to pizza. I expect you and Alex to be there too."

Although Kaylene smiled and thanked her, a shiver of loneliness made her sad. Only Alex's promise of love could exorcise it forever. She tried to enjoy the others' company and pay attention to the game.

For a group of women who had given her all the negative aspects of life with a coach, they were wildly enthusiastic team supporters. Without referring to the printed programs, they knew player names and cheered individual efforts. They yelled at the referees for poor judgment and created their own version of pep squad cheers with their giggling children. Everyone shared in the excitement of success as Leon Creek scored two touchdowns within the first quarter.

Kaylene enjoyed being included in the spirited fun. Although she watched Alex's games with interest because she knew the coach and the players, the camaraderie among the wives who shared the wins and losses together was a new aspect she hadn't considered as part of Alex's life as a coach. Two weeks ago, she had overreacted to the disappointed mood of the coaches and the critical response of their wives. So caught up in the negative atmosphere, she didn't realize the women relied on one another for support during the tough times, but shared good times too.

After the game, which Leon Creek won, 21-14, Kaylene declined Gloria's invitation to eat pizza with everyone. She decided she would go home, and formulate what she would tell Alex. Now that she had tackled her fears, it was time to create a winning strategy for their relationship.

—␣␣␣—

Saturday's game topped the charts for frustration, aggravation, and bad calls by the officials.

Alex could hardly keep his temper under control. Instead, he rammed his fingers through his curly hair. *Where did David find these refs anyway? Couldn't they tell the different between a fumble and a dead ball?*

Hector's knee was down before the ball came loose. This turnover couldn't have come at a worse time.

He yelled to his defensive line running onto the field. "Come on, now! Hold 'em! Don't let them score!" Under his breath, he muttered a very unsportsmanlike word as he saw the referees spot the ball on Leon Creek's twelve-yard line. As the muscles in his stomach tightened, he wondered if he'd have ulcers before he was thirty.

Each time the ball snapped, and his team kept McCullum from scoring, Alex's nerves seemed to boomerang over the field. Despite the three failed attempts, the McCullum coach decided not to punt, but go for the first down.

This time the opposition scored. From across the field, Alex could hear the victorious cheers. Jerking his shoulder as if he shrugged off the disappointment, he clapped his hands. "Come on, now! Block that kick!"

The triumph of blocking the kick was a temporary lift. Unfortunately, the game ended before Leon Creek had time to score another touchdown. Final score: 20-14.

Alex strode across the field to congratulate the McCullum coach, then turned around to meet his boys for his post-game talk. He knew his boys played their best, and he had every intention of telling them he was proud of their work today.

His eyes raised from the boys on the sidelines to sweep the bleachers. Then, he saw the brunette hair blowing in the breeze, the familiar red jacket, and shapely legs in tight blue jeans.

The sight of Kaylene filled him with apprehension. Suddenly he felt like a field-goal kicker who had to kick the ball and break a tie. Was there a chance to win after all?

—⁂—

Kaylene zipped up her red jacket. The autumn day was crisp and cold, but the beauty of bright sunshine and clear skies was lost on the boys kneeling around their coaches as they talked about the game. She heard the buzz of Alex's voice, low and solemn.

She walked down the bleachers. There was so much she yearned to discuss with Alex. But how did she invite him to her apartment for lunch without someone overhearing and adding the information to further school gossip?

Slowly, she walked along the grass beneath the bleachers and waited by the railing.

"Hi, Miss Morales," a few of the freshmen players greeted as they passed her, heading for the gym.

"We'll get them next time," one of them said with a shy smile.

These boys—Alex's team—weren't ready to give up on themselves. She admired their optimism and knew it was because a coach like Alex Garrison believed in them.

She responded with a cheerful, "I know you will."

Kaylene heard Domingo's voice, "I'll take care of the boys, Alex," only seconds before Alex stood in front of her. She was surprised to see him smiling when his team had just lost a difficult game.

"I'm glad to see you." He reached out and took her hand.

Her eyes darted nervously, but she relaxed when she saw all the boys had gone into the gym. "I'm sorry your team lost the game."

"I heard what happened in sixth period yesterday."

She felt a blush spreading over her face. "Word gets around fast, doesn't it? Everyone seems to be talking about us."

"Yes, I know. Ralph Hernandez has a lot of friends."

Slowly, Kaylene raised her eyes and stared into his. She expected to see disappointment from losing the game, but all she saw was that same friendly warmth she had known since she was a teenager.

"Alex, we have so many things to talk about."

"So, talk. I'm listening."

"But what about your team?"

"Domingo can handle them. You're more important right now."

His hands tightened on hers. He had said the words she had hoped to hear.

"Do you mean that, Alex?"

"Kaylene, I love you. I can't tell you what my life's been like the past two weeks. I wanted to call you, to see you, but I knew it wouldn't be fair. I just hoped you'll tell me there's still a chance for us."

"Alex, the one thing I want to tell you is that I love you. You're very important to me."

"But I'm still a coach."

"Then I'll have to share you with the team during football season. I know I can do that now."

Alex pulled her into his arms. He was her safe haven after two weeks of drifting on a sea of doubts and fears. She breathed deeply, inhaling his scent, then raised her face to brush her cheek against his. Everything felt so familiar and so wonderful. She didn't want to let him go, but she loved him enough to let him return to his responsibilities as a coach.

"I think you'd better get back to your team."

His throaty chuckle was a happy melody to her ears.

"My love, someday you're going to make a great coach's wife!"

Kaylene pulled back to study his expression. His grayish-green eyes held the gleam of his laugh, and the promise of their own version of *happily ever after.*

A slow smile spread over her face. "Do you really mean that?"

"Excuse me, Alex!" A loud deep voice sailed between them.

Kaylene dropped her arms, as Alex turned to face David Maldonado, about three feet away from them. Big hands on his hips, the head coach kicked at the ground, scuffing the toe of his white tennis shoes. "Sorry to interrupt, Coach, but I need to talk to you."

When Alex stepped away, Kaylene felt chilled.

The serious expression on David's face told her inviting Alex to her apartment for lunch would be futile. Was there more broken equipment? Or did the head coach need Alex to explain something on a scouting report? She tried to keep the disappointment off her face. She had just told Alex she could share him more during the football season, and now seemed to facing another test.

"I need you to go to Laredo tonight," David said.

"Laredo?" Alex's eyebrows raised. "Tonight?"

"Yes. Floresville's playing there tonight. I already talked to Johnson and Perez. They'll meet you here at three."

Listening to this conversation, Kaylene stared at her boots. Alex was going to leave again before she could really explain her feelings about the two of them.

There was a long silence before Alex said, "I'll go, David, but the others have to take their own car."

His tone reminded Kaylene of the first day they met. But Kaylene didn't blame Alex for making those demands after what happened in Carrizo Springs. He probably wanted to travel in a car he trusted.

"And, David—I won't be driving back tonight. I'll need to stay in Laredo and drive back tomorrow. So, don't expect me at the meeting until noon."

Kaylene looked at Alex, surprised and shocked by the way he made his intentions known to his head coach. Then Alex shocked her even more when he slipped his arm around her shoulders. "Kaylene's parents live in Laredo, David. I need to get re-acquainted. I'm hoping to marry their daughter next year."

A soft gasp escaped her, surprised again by this unpredictable man.

When Alex pulled her around to face him, she forgot about David entirely.

Alex's eyes sparkled as he smiled gently. "Have any plans for tonight, Kaylene?"

"I think I'm going to Laredo," she said in a voice that seemed to come from a long way off.

His lips touched hers for a brief moment. "We'll love each other regardless of the season. Do you like that idea?"

"Yes," she whispered, then kissed him again. Her eyes fastened on the goalposts behind him. They had made their own touchdown, a touchdown for love. The victory was worth the sacrifice.

About the Author

Diane Gonzales Bertrand began writing novels when she was in fifth grade at Little Flower School in San Antonio, Texas. She continued by writing humorous plays for her drama class, poetry for her relatives, and skits for Girl Scout camp. After graduating from the University of Texas at San Antonio in 1979, she began teaching English at St. Paul's School and Holy Cross High School. She also continued writing poetry, plays for her students to perform, and religious prayers and ceremonies. She started writing for publication after she earned her graduate degree in English-Communication Arts from Our Lady of the Lake University in 1992. She wanted to see women like herself portrayed in literature and wrote stories like she wanted to read. Her recent books from Piñata Books include *Sweet Fifteen*, a novel about the celebration of a *quinceañera; Alicia's Treasure*, a novel for younger readers; and the picture book *Sip, Slurp, Soup, Soup/ Caldo, Caldo, Caldo*. She is currently working on new picture books and novels for students in middle school.

Ms. Bertrand still lives in San Antonio with her husband, Nick, and their two children. She teaches creative writing and English composition at St. Mary's University, and she presents creative writing workshops to children, teens, and adults in schools and libraries across Texas.

Author's Note

This novel was recently revised from the original version, which was titled *Touchdown for Love*. While the characters and their conflicts remain essentially the same, the narrative and dialogue have been revised and updated. I appreciate the support from the entire team at Arte Público Press. They realized the importance of republishing this story for the many young people who have enjoyed my other books. I also wish to thank my two writing friends Carla Joinson and Audrey Elliot, who guided me through the revision process. Finally, I re-dedicate this novel to my husband Nick C. Bertrand, the man who fills my life with love and laughter.